RIDGEVILLE SERIES VOLUME I

Table of Contents

HE AIN'T LION 1
    Chapter One 3
    Chapter Two 18
    Chapter Three 46
    Chapter Four 57
    Chapter Five 70
    Chapter Six 83
YOU'RE LION 96
BALL OF FURRY 141
    Prologue 143
    Chapter One 157
    Chapter Two 184
    Chapter Three 203
    Chapter Four 224
    Chapter Five 239
    Epilogue 262
About Celia Kyle 273
Copyright Page 274

HE AIN'T LION

Chapter One

Alex O'Connell watched the ripple of awareness ease through Genesis, his club, as each male seemingly became mindful of the newcomer, the unknown human female, in their midst. The singular woman who smelled nothing of pride or pack.

Shit, fuck, damn, and growl.

He ran a hand through his hair and willed his inner cat to calm. Unfortunately, the beast wasn't in the mood to be denied. It'd already scented the lush woman, and was more than ready to pounce—strip her naked and slide his hard length inside her body.

How the fuck had she gained entrance?

The semiannual Gaian Moon was making an appearance tonight, so Alex had gathered his pride and willing humans, known as familiars, to converge within the confines of the club. Sex could be had, raucous noises could be made, and most of the furniture had already been cat-proofed.

Who was she, this unfamiliar female swaying her curvaceous hips amongst his felines, completely oblivious to the trouble she was about to cause?

The Gaian Moon ensured cubs would be born, and that their pride would continue to flourish. Without the celestial rising their numbers would almost certainly dwindle, and they'd likely wither and die, as true matings were extremely rare among his kind.

The humans in attendance knew what they were in for, the moment they'd become pride familiars. The pride would care for them and any offspring, for the remainder of their lives, so long as they made themselves available at the Gaian Moon gatherings, and helped the pride when called upon. Giving birth to cubs only ensured that pride protection and support would be everlasting.

There were several true matings in their pride, but those couples remained at home to make little cubs of their own, while the others romped their way through Genesis.

The female in the tight, cleavage-revealing red dress, though, was not a familiar. Alex knew this, because he was the prime, damn it.

Shit, fuck, damn, and growl.

His felines were staring at her as if she was a slaughtered deer, and they hadn't eaten for weeks. Even so, she continued to mingle, now easily fifty feet from where he stood, and yet, he could still scent her heat, single her out from amongst the gatherers. He needed to do something. Fast.

"You need to do something, Alex. And fast." Grayson's words cut through his thoughts, mirroring his own. "She's not one of ours."

"I know." Alex barely recognized his own voice, and he paused for a moment to take stock of his body's responses to the new arrival. His cat, normally easy to control after years of practice, was fighting Alex's restraint, snarling and snapping at its internal cage, prowling just beneath the thin veneer of his skin. The fucker wanted out. Now.

His arms tingled, skin prickled, and he knew—without looking—that golden fur had sprouted from his forearms. The throbbing from his hands would soon reveal fuzzy fingers, and lethal, razor-sharp claws. Fuckity fuck.

"How'd she get in?" His lengthened canines made speech difficult, but not impossible.

He watched the expressions that flitted across his second's face, where feelings of regret and remorse appeared to be dueling for supremacy. "I put Gina on the door, and she said she could've *sworn* the woman was on the list. And that her scent held your mark."

Alex rolled his eyes, immediately refocusing his gaze on the tempting interloper. Her blonde hair practically glowed under the dim lights of the club, her pale skin a beacon his lion was more than happy to follow to the ends of the earth. "She's still pissed at me for not mounting her during the last moon, and I'm sure she's just itching to start some trouble."

Grayson nodded. "I think you may be right."

Lion wanted this stranger. No doubt about its feelings, the beast practically begged and snarled its needs to Alex. Part of him wanted to charge through the gathering, steal her away to his den. Unfortunately he couldn't do that, not without revealing his true nature to the woman. Sure, shifters were known to the human populace, but they weren't exactly "out and proud" about their existence. Nonchalance and some closely kept secrets had kept the shifters protected thus far, and the various clan leaders around the world wanted to keep it that way.

Alex had too much on his plate already, and he'd rather not add "calming a panicking human" to the list.

"Bring her up, Grayson. I'll speak with her, and then send her on her way. Perhaps give her an incentive to return on another night. We can't have her in the building once the doors are locked and the festivities have begun."

"There's only five minutes left, Prime."

As if the reminder of his title within the pride wasn't enough to pressure him, the last thing Alex needed was to be further stressed by his second's announcement of the remaining time, damn it. His cat was more than aware of how long it needed to wait until it could mate with the fertile, willing females, and the opportunity to produce cubs of its own, true mate or not. His lion had yet to be successful, but it was more than willing to keep trying... "Then make it fast."

*

Her friend Gina hadn't lied. The guys in Genesis were all staring at her as if she were a big hunk of choice beef, and they hadn't eaten for weeks. Then again, the whole semi-drooling thing could be because they were werecats. But wait, weren't dogs the droolers?

Maya mentally shrugged. Gina, even if she did seem a little cat crazy, was fun to hang out with, and now, she was Maya's very best, hook-me-up-with-hotness, friend.

She'd known all along that shifters lived in Ridgeville, as well as many of the surrounding towns in their wide expanse of North Carolina, so the all-cat club and semiannual orgy didn't really surprise her much. She'd always heard that shifters were very sexual beings.

And tonight, she could very well use some of that sexual healing.

Heh.

The men here certainly seemed to like a girl with some cushion for the pushin'. At least, that's what their gazes told her. Hell, even some of the ladies were giving Maya the same lustful glances. But tonight was not the night for lovin' with the female persuasion, though. Maybe another time...

Maya wove her way through the crush of bodies, trying to ignore the occasional brushes against her, casual touches that roamed from her hips to her ass, and sometimes the side of her breasts.

Yet another thing her new friend hadn't lied about. It seemed these men were into fluffy women. Maya was a realist, she always had been. She had big hips, big thighs, and big breasts, all of which added up to a big woman.

Whatever. 'Cause she was perfectly content with who she was.

And by all appearances the men liked what they saw, and she just wanted to have a fun night on the town, forget about her ex's betrayal and hateful words. It'd been a month since the blowup breakup, and it was high time for her to shake off the remnants of Henry's mistreatment of her and reclaim her life.

The first order of business was a debauchery-filled night at Genesis, where, to her knowledge, no one knew her as the other half of "Maya and Henry".

Gina had told her that the club held a sex party of sorts every six months. It was a "cat" thing so it wasn't advertised, but people in the know gathered here to have a bit of fun. Were werecats considered "people?"

Maya wasn't much of an exhibitionist, but her new friend's persuasive words had convinced her that a trip to Genesis would be the first step to reclaiming her life—the whole "sexual healing" part of her plan.

As she approached the bar a few of the men first seemed to part like the Red Sea, but then crowded closer, with one on each side, and she could feel the presence of at least two others at her back. And their hard cocks were not lost on her.

She should totally be disgusted. Really. 'Cause normal "good girls" wouldn't get turned-on by being surrounded by a handful of werecats, with boinking on their minds, would they?

In truth, their blatant desire sent a thrill down her spine, settling nicely in her pussy, causing her needy clit to twitch.

Any other time she would've glared at them all or perhaps even called the cops, but not as of this moment, when glancing at each man revealed large bodies with heated stares, pale, amber eyes that just oozed sex.

And she sure as hell wouldn't kick any of them outta bed.

When she turned her attention back to the bar, she found the mixologist staring at her, sex and seduction obvious in his heavy-lidded gaze, while his focus seemed trained on her ample breasts.

"Can I help you, Miss?" His soothing voice wrapped around her, and she could feel her sex growing wetter, aching with want and prepping for a night of naughty fun as she took her seat.

The men crowded closer, capturing her with their bodies, chests rubbing and touching, random hands petting, and she couldn't think of a single reason to push them away. No, tonight, she'd be a wanton sex goddess. Okay, that sounded kinda lame. Rather, she'd be a horny slut.

Just for this single night.

One. No harm, no foul.

Maya *definitely* wouldn't return in six months, though.

Nope.

Well, *maybe*.

If she were invited, sure, probably.

A low growl flitted on the room's breeze, a moment before a man spoke in a commanding voice from behind her. "No, you cannot."

And just that quickly, the men surrounding her melted away, the mixologist doing the same but in the opposite direction, moving toward other customers in haste.

A glance to her left and right revealed that she suddenly had a generous, five-foot radius of personal space.

Maya turned on her stool, faced the man who'd sent her suitors running, but immediately tossed out all of her aggravation that stemmed from the other men deserting her. 'Cause she'd be more than happy to take this man on, considering how insistent and growly he happened to be. *Yummy.*

This guy appeared to be taller than the others, an air of authority wrapped around him, and she wondered what it'd be like to be taken by him, bent over the bar and...fucked senseless.

He approached, a predator clothed in skin. And she seemed to be his prey.

"Ma'am, if you'll come with me..." He held out a large hand, and she wondered what it'd be like to be touched and stroked by him, forced to come over and again until he shoved what she hoped would be a large dick into her heat.

A small shudder shook her body, lower lips growing heavy with desire as his nostrils flared, chest expanding when he inhaled deep, the hue of his amber eyes growing deeper with each flurried beat of her racing heart.

Definitely a big cat. Most definitely. And it was obvious that he could scent her longing. That should've squicked her out. Without a doubt.

But it didn't.

Huh.

Oh, was she ready for the festivities to begin. She slid from her stool, a slight wobble when she gained her feet, her new stilettos giving her grief. She totally should've gone with three-inch heels instead of four.

The hottie was there in a blink, arm wrapped around her waist, a steadying hand encircling her wrist. "Are you okay? Have you had a lot to drink?"

She furrowed her eyebrows and puckered her lips into a pout. "*No.*" She kept pace with him as they wove through the club, men and women moving aside as they approached. "You scared him away, before I had the chance to order."

The stranger leaned down, nuzzled her neck and inhaled, before he purred in her ear, "Sorry."

Holy shit, oh, dear God, please take her now. He hadn't touched her yet, not really, but she already wanted this man. Wanted to be spread over a table and taken by him, and she couldn't give a flying fuck who watched. No, she'd just charge for admittance.

At the bottom of a set of stairs she found her voice. "Where're you taking me?"

"Alex O'Connell, the owner of Genesis, would like to meet you." Damn. There was that lovely purr again.

Okay, she could certainly do that. Maya wasn't exactly an "in the know" regular, so meeting him was probably a good idea. She wasn't sure if hosting orgies in clubs was all that legal in Ridgeville, so meeting a random newcomer without a direct invite kinda made sense. Besides, Gina had warned her that she might have to chat with the head honcho before the fun began at midnight.

Maybe she shoulda brought catnip along, as a peace offering or something.

She licked her lips, stole another look at her escort, and wondered if she could finagle him into a bit of slap-and-tickle, and then, a thorough, hard fucking.

And plenty of it.

Before she knew it they were at the top of the stairs, her escort knocking on the wooden door.

One rap is all he managed until the door opened, an obviously livid man standing on the other side, his face a ruddy hue, and eyes that looked ready to shoot daggers at her at any moment. And if it weren't for the teeny-tiny fact that his face held an expression that indicated he'd gladly end her life without a second thought, she'd drool all over him, drop to her knees and beg to touch him, be touched by him.

"Grayson, you took your time." The man spoke through clenched teeth.

Oh. Oh, my. While her escort, Grayson, had gotten her warm in all the right places, this man, Alex O'Connell, made her want in a way she'd never experienced.

Even with his thunderous expression she wasn't afraid, not really. Grayson held an air of authority, while this man personified power. It radiated from him, but for some odd reason, she felt like he wouldn't really harm her. He demanded, and others listened. But he also seemed to have a fierce level of control.

"Yes, apparently, I did."

Maya didn't have eyes for Grayson any longer. No, she was all about Mr. Alex O'Connell and his bad self. He easily topped six feet, and then some. His hair appeared reddish-blond in color, and seemed to shine in the dim club interior. As did his eyes. Oh, damn, his eyes were the palest amber, and held something she couldn't quite describe. It called to her on a primal level, all of her instincts screaming at her to climb him like a freaking mountain and never come back down.

But fluffy chicks, especially her, were not climbers.

Alex's shoulders were so broad he nearly spanned the doorway, and they led to an equally wide chest which tapered to a trim waist. His shirt was so tight she could see the ripple of every muscle when he moved, count each dip and rise along his abdomen. The black top matched the snug pants that revealed just as much as they hid. She couldn't help but steal a glance at the juncture of his thighs, nearly gasping as the large package grew beneath her gaze, showing her, that despite his anger, she turned him on.

Thank god. Her body was responding too, whether she liked it or not. Good thing momma liked.

Beneath his attention her nipples pebbled and hardened within her dress, and how appropriate, because she wasn't wearing a bra that could hide the effects of his impassioned stare. The arousal didn't stop with her breasts, though. It slithered through her body, awakening and strumming her nerves as it wove its way to her aching pussy, flicking her clit as her wet channel clenched in response. A shiver struck her muscles and she imagined his thick cock sliding, and then slamming, into her body. Powerful. Hard. Fast.

Alex took a deep breath and his nostrils flared, mimicking Grayson's actions from before, his fierce anger melting into an even more ferocious expression she could only interpret as hard core, wanna-do-you-now-so-stop-touching-my-friend-and-bend-over, lust.

Whew.

Yes, please.

"That'll be all." Alex snapped the words out as he reached for her, pulled her out of Grayson's arms and hauled her into his apparent sanctuary, then closed the door once the man left.

With the need and desire to be bent over any flat surface lingering, she couldn't really find the energy, or inclination, to care about his aggressive behavior.

Maya came to Genesis to help take her mind off of Henry, but this...and these feelings...were completely foreign, unexpected. When she was deciding whether or not to come, she'd figured she'd get turned-on, have a little fun, and then leave, once the "thank you, ma'am" of the "wham, bam" portion of the night came to pass.

Now, she wasn't all that sure that if she was to get a taste of Alex...that once would be enough.

He led her deeper into the room and she got the impression of dark wood, masculine furniture, but he didn't give her a chance to look around. Within a few steps he had her captured, with her leaning against the back of the sofa while he loomed over her, his rock-hard erection pressed against her hips.

"What's your name?" His mouth hovered near hers, his heated breath fanning her skin. Close enough to kiss, but he didn't close the distance.

"Maya." She licked her lips, mouth and throat dry. "Maya Josephs."

He leaned forward and she thought he would kiss her, take her mouth and show her his skills. No, he only nuzzled the line of her jaw, just below her ear, continuing on until his face was pressed against the juncture of her neck and shoulder. He inhaled deep, brushing her nipples with his chest, causing her pussy to tighten, causing more of her cream to dampen her already wet panties. When he exhaled his warm breath teased her skin, with more of her need pouring through her, her arousal rising even higher.

A groan sounded from his chest and he pressed closer still, his form aligned with hers from chest to knees, allowing her to feel his body's responses.

This felt too good to be bad, and though she really wasn't the kind of girl to open her legs for a guy from the get-go, she'd be lyin' if that hadn't been her plan for the night.

It most certainly was.

"Maya..." He sounded tortured, aroused, yet torn. "I should make you leave. Right now. This instant."

Maya whimpered, rocked her hips against Alex's, hoping she could be enough of a temptress so he wouldn't send her away. Because... He was like a twelve on the fuck-me-now scale. "No...please...don't."

She hadn't been able to keep Henry in her bed, not with her curves and "fat" body, but she hoped she could lure Alex just a bit further. Okay, a lot further, since she wanted him naked and fucking her before the night was over.

"My sweet, you shouldn't stay. You don't understand." His voice sounded deeper, rougher, and needy as hell.

"I'm a big girl, Alex." She almost snorted at the pun. *Almost.* "One night." She reached between them, stroked his cloth-covered dick from top to bottom and back again, making sure she squeezed and pressed while she pet him. "I'm not asking for anything more. Just this one night..."

He moved his hands, face still buried against her neck, breathing deep as he caressed her arms, fingers trailing over her exposed skin, his teasing touch leaving goose bumps in its wake. At the top of her dress he traced the edge, then over her breasts, making her gasp.

"You don't know what a sweet temptation you are, Maya." He hooked his finger beneath the hem and tugged, exposing more of her abundant flesh and nipples to the cool air.

She whimpered, aching and needing more of his pleasurable touch. "Alex..."

Yes, she had a good chance of winning the "Slut of the Year" award this time around. No doubt. But as far as she knew, one-nighters were supposed to be all about the quick fuck. So yeah, she probably was doing something right.

Another pull and she thought she heard the tearing of cloth, but then he cupped one of her bare breasts, thumb tracing her hard nubbin', and she couldn't give a flying fuck if he'd ripped her dress. She'd steal a club t-shirt before she left if need be. Plus, there were other dresses in the world to be had, but there was only one Alex, and only this night to be with him. She was quite sure of that.

Here kitty, kitty...

Chapter Two

Alex knew he should let her go, shove her out the front door and maybe hunt her down later...when his beast wasn't riding him so hard, demanding that he claim the female in his arms, and produce lots of little cubs for him to protect. But he simply couldn't.

Just because her lush body and intoxicating scent called to his lion and him like no other had before, it didn't mean he could do as he pleased and munch on an unsuspecting human. Yeah, shifters were known about, but the world didn't know everything... Didn't know about their mating, the moon, the turning of people...none of it.

But all his cat wanted to do was roll around in her scent, and make sure they stayed tangled until they smelled as one. Fuck, the idea made his cock throb in his jeans, and just as it did, her tiny hand squeezed between his legs again, immediately eliciting a moan from him.

"Maya..." He shifted his hold, pinched and rolled her nipple, absorbing every whimper from her lips and reveling in her satisfying response.

She arched into his touch, as if pressing her lush tit into his possession. "Please..."

Oh, fuck. He couldn't resist a begging woman, especially not one his beast ached to claim as its own. At the thought of claiming, pain lanced through his gums, his canines extending within his mouth, while a deep, bestial growl formed in his chest. Shit, the beast within badly wanted her. Good thing the man did, too.

With a groan he dropped to his knees, his mouth at the perfect height to suckle her nipples. She was such a pretty thing, and all he wanted to do was wrap her in cotton and keep her safe for...ever. She would be his. She just didn't know it yet. It was only now that he was beginning to see it for himself.

Alex wasted no time in capturing a nipple, sucking the nub into his mouth and flicking it with his tongue. With his other hand he kneaded the other heavy mound, pinching gently on the firm nubbin'.

In moments the heady scent of her arousal surrounded him, wrapped around his cock like a living thing, jerking the hard shaft aching between his thighs. He kissed his way to her other nipple, treated it with the same attention as he did the first, scraping one of his canines over her sensitive skin, growling when she sifted her fingers through his hair. Lion wanted to sink its teeth into the softness of her skin, claiming Maya while passion rode them hard. It'd never heard of a mating mark being placed on a woman's breast, but his lion didn't seem to give a damn, either.

She pulled him against her chest, forced more of her flesh into his mouth, and in turn, he gave her what she seemed to be demanding. The beast wanted to please its mate, wanted to provide whatever she desired.

The man ignored the "mate" part of his lion's thoughts. Alex wanted her just as much as his inner cat, but letting those thoughts linger would only snag his attention away from controlling the snarls roaring inside his head.

The impatient beast was not happy. It wanted her. And now.

Alex let her nipple drop from his mouth with a pop, and raised his gaze to meet hers. A satisfied smile split his lips when he saw her passion, her heavy-lidded eyes and blatant need dancing over her beautiful features. Arousal made her skin flushed, and those well-loved breasts had pinked from his heated attention. He wanted to bite every inch of her ivory skin, leave his mark to show the other males that this female belonged to him.

The musky scent of her cream taunted him, lured him closer and closer to the juncture of her thighs. While he'd toyed with her lush breasts she'd widened her stance, the bottom part of her dress stretched taut between her thick thighs.

Squatting down he leaned forward, bending his head, pressing his chin just above her mound, rubbing it back and forth. His gaze focused on her, Alex intently watched for her reaction. The fabric kept them separated, but he knew the pressure would still give her some pleasure.

Maya gasped and shuddered, rocked her hips against his touch. "Oh, Alex..."

Keeping his chin in place, he taunted, "What do you need, sweet? I'll give you anything, just say the words."

"Please..." She bit her lip, her eyes rolling into the back of her head, and she tensed against him once more. "Will you...lick me? There?"

Alex leaned back and brought his hands to her knees, slid his palms along the outside of her thick legs, bringing the silky, barely-there material with him. Within moments the tops of her thighs were revealed to him. So plump and curvy that he couldn't wait to have them wrapped around his waist, holding him close while he buried his dick into her tight heat.

But first...

"Lick you where, Maya?" The cat knew. Lion wanted to lap at her cream, gather up every drop of her juices into its mouth. He could see her arousal creeping through her silken panties. Saw the damp spot grow larger before his eyes. "Do you want me to eat this pretty little pussy of yours? Hm?"

She whimpered and nodded, her lip tucked between her teeth.

"Say the words for me." Alex leaned forward and tested his resolve. He licked at the wet bit of cloth and let his eyes drift closed while he savored her taste. Her essence held the flavors of vanilla, musk, and an aromatic sweetness his inner cat just wanted to drown in.

Alex agreed. He repeated the action, brushed the fabric just hard enough to yank a groan from her.

"Lick my...pussy. Pretty please, Alex?

*

Maya froze for a moment, surprised by her own audacious behavior. Those thoughts, those words, typically lived in her mind. Deep inside. Like a subterranean mole rooted in the back of her brain. She'd always fantasized about talking dirty, about directing her lover, but Henry had always preferred her to be quiet.

But with Alex on the other hand... Oh, god, it felt wonderful, talking and begging something awful to the man at her feet, watching his eyes darken with each syllable she spoke. His thumbs teased the outsides of her hips and inner thighs, dancing along the edge of her panties, so close to where she needed him, yet so far.

The delicate touch aroused her even further, her clit aching, hurting with the desire to be stroked and licked. Her pussy felt empty, desperate to be filled with his cock, over and over again.

This is what Gina had promised she would find here, and Maya was damned thankful that Genesis had delivered.

From the look on Alex's face, Maya figured cats had a real thing for cream. No, she'd never dated or had sex with a shifter, but she had no doubt the man at her feet was all cat. His amber eyes had turned into a fiery gold, and she could've sworn his arms were sporting a bit more golden hair than before.

Good. From the gossip she'd heard, that meant this guy was really into her. But all she wanted was for him to be *inside* her.

Alex didn't make her ask again, didn't make her repeat the words. No, he slid his hands further up her thighs until he could grasp the waist of her panties again, and then tugged them down her legs, helped her kick them aside.

The cool air of the room wafted over her soaking pussy, causing goose bumps to rise on her legs. She turned her focus to him, watched while he stroked the juncture of her thighs with his thumbs.

Oh, she'd never seen a man look so hungry, so intent on her before. No...never like this. His eyes practically shone in the dim room, licking his lips as if he were being presented with a feast.

"*Please?*" Maya had never thought she'd beg a man for his touch, but she'd obviously been wrong.

He spared her a glance, gifted her with a smirk and a wink, just before he repositioned his hold, carefully spreading her lower lips. "Damn, sweet. You're so fucking pink and hot for me, aren't you? Fuck, I need to taste you. "

Alex leaned forward and she couldn't have torn her attention away if she'd wanted to. His tongue snaked out and touched the very top of her slit, lapped and pet the sensitive bit of her mons, and she automatically whimpered in response, letting the sofa fully take her weight.

"Mm...you taste so good." His voice was deep, a near growl, but she didn't care. Not when he came back for more, not when the flat of his coarse tongue rubbed over her aching clit, sending another burst of pleasure through her body.

He took his time, licking, tasting, laving her pussy with expert strokes. When he wasn't gathering her cream around her opening and swallowing it down, he was nibbling the aroused flesh, tiny bites of her labia, a scrape of a tooth against her clit. And yeah, it was a big fucking tooth.

Here kitty, kitty...

"Yes, Alex...just like that." She curled her fingers into his hair, holding on while he gave her the most pleasure she'd ever experienced.

Henry had been...adequate. Alex was extraordinary.

He brought his tongue from the top of her slit and down to her heat before going back again, moaning and growling deep against her flesh. Each of his animalistic sounds sent vibrations through her pussy, and a shiver of ecstasy along her spine.

Maya brought her free hand to her breast, kneaded the plump flesh and tugged on her hardened nipple.

Alex turned his attention from her soaking cunt and focused on her, their gazes clashing, locking into one. "Want you to come on my face, sweet. Can you do that for me?"

Oh, god, she was a slut of epic proportions. At least, she knew his name and where he worked. That had to diminish her chances for receiving the "Slut of the Year" award, right? Maybe make her a runner-up?

She nodded, watched while he brushed her clit with his thumb, and she couldn't hold back her responses to his delicate touch. Her whole body twitched and spasmed, back arching and trembling with the fierce shot of lightning-laced pleasure that stimulated her nerves.

"Oh, someone likes that, don't they?" He chuckled, bringing his mouth back to her pussy, but leaving his thumb in place.

That wonderfully torturous digit of his...

He circled her clit, round and round and round again, teased her with his strokes while he lapped at her hole. With each pass of his tongue her pussy clenched and released more cream, bathing his face in her juices.

And Alex seemed to love it. He growled, pressed closer, tongue fucking her hole as if he were hell-bent on sending her over the edge. Wondrous sounds continued to travel from his mouth to her aroused heat, ratcheting her need higher and higher with each passing second.

He growled, she twitched. He moaned, she gasped.

The hottest man she knew in her life was between her thighs, eating her like she was a buffet, and she couldn't get enough of him.

Alex quit his gentle teasing, the circling of her pussy with his tongue, and slipped a finger into her sopping cunt.

"Fuck!" Maya grasped the edge of the couch for support.

"Yeah, sweet. In due time. Just as soon as you come for me."

She trembled, rocked her hips against his delightful invasion. Alex kept that talented thumb circling her clit, a nice and steady rhythm that promised to deliver on his demand. "T-Two."

"Hm? Oh...got it." He pulled the single finger free and replaced it with two, the thick invasion stretching her pussy the tiniest bit.

"Yes!" Her pussy clamped down, thankful to be filled with more of him, even if it wasn't his cock.

Fuck, she wanted. Wanted him to slam those fingers in and out of her pussy, make her come and cream all over him, before he bent her over the couch and took her fast and hard.

As if he'd read her mind, he did exactly that.

Alex pumped in and out of her hole, nice and slow at first, and then his tempo changed, his fingers moved faster, pushed deeper, and his thumb mirrored the pace as it massaged her clit. God, the man knew how to get a woman to come. Ladies didn't need fancy tricks. No, all they needed was a nice consistent fucking, with no random movements. Slow and steady won the race.

Maya shifted her hips, worked to meet each thrust, trying desperately to increase her pleasure. Her orgasm was rapidly approaching, dancing and running closer to the edge with each brush of his thumb, each press of his fingers into her wet heat.

And then...

And then he changed his penetration, did something with his fingers and touched a sweet spot inside her pussy that yanked a scream from her throat. "Alex!"

"Found it, didn't I?" She felt his breath fan over her sopping pussy.

She pried her eyes open, watched him plunge his fingers in and out of her slick heat, a predatory smile on his face the entire time he finger fucked her.

"Ohfuckohfuckohfuck..." Maya pinched her nipples, tugged and gave herself a bit of pain to mingle with the pleasure coursing throughout her stimulated body.

Her orgasm gathered strength, twirling, twisting, turning inside her, breezing over her singing nerves and lighting them with her burning arousal. Mouth barely open she panted, turned-on by his fingers plundering her cunt, and the lewd display he presented for her to watch.

Alex's lips and chin shone with her juices, while his eyes turned into the darkest color of gold. She thought she saw the hard line of his dick in his pants, like it was more than ready to delve deep inside her. The sprinkles of fur that she'd glimpsed before now coated his forearms, glowing and glittering in the low light.

God, she'd never experienced anything so decadent, so thrilling. A man, more beast than anything, desired her above the other gorgeous women in the club. He drooled over her curvy body. Again, did cats drool?

Apparently, they did.

"Give it to me, Maya." His voice had dipped inexplicably deeper, almost an animalistic growl that echoed throughout the empty room.

Maya couldn't deny him, couldn't hold back her body's response to his demand. She arched, dropped her head back and let her orgasm gather, the bubble of pleasure growing larger with every breath she took, each press of his fingers and rub of his thumb over her clit egging her climax along. It formed like a balloon within her body, increasing in size with each quick beat of her pounding heart. Her pussy clenched and milked his intrusion, body shuddering and twitching with each circle over her clit.

God, she couldn't breathe, couldn't think past the building pleasure that skipped and danced along her spine, then centering on her pussy, sending tendrils of bliss through her arms and legs. She was a giant ball of fire, blazing uncontrollably higher and bigger, reacting every bit to Alex's touch.

"G-Gonna..."

The word left her lips a mere second before she felt like she'd shattered, splintered into a million pieces as she came around his fingers, milking him, pussy spasming, each twitch shooting yet another burst of pleasure through her tensing body. She thrashed and jerked while wave after wave of rapture ignited every one of her nerves.

The orgasm slipped and slithered through her, her muscles tensing while Alex gradually slowed his masterful movements. He brought her down in tiny increments, until her legs could barely hold her weight, her knees nearly jelly-like.

Through slitted eyes she watched her shifter lover pull his fingers free of her cunt, and then slip them into his mouth, moaning almost joyfully around his digits. With a pop he released them, and rolled to his feet.

"Damn, sweet. You're delicious."

Before she could respond he captured her lips and thrust his tongue into her mouth, tangling his with hers. She stiffened at his initial invasion, but then melted into him, savored the taste of her cream mixed with his masculine flavor, her musk mingling with the naturally occurring citrus and cinnamon that marked him.

He notched his dick against her still exposed pussy, rubbed the ridge of his cock along her sensitive slit as she clung to his shoulders, before wrapping her legs around his waist, pulling him flush against her needy cunt.

He growled and then moaned at the contact, ground his hips over her, yanking a whimper from deep within. Her channel clenched on air, practically begging to be filled with him, his fingers, his cock, anything that was an extension of him.

Large hands slid over her hips, then reached around to cup and knead her ass. God she needed this, needed the touch of a man who wanted her for who exactly who she was. Alex, this stranger of all people, seemed to be the one to do just that. Suddenly, Maya was lifted from the back of the couch, and in a split-second, her world began to spin.

"Alex!" She struggled against his hold. The man was strong, but she was...fluffy. "I'm too heavy. Put me down!"

He paused a moment to glare at her, and she could've sworn his eyes flashed bright, before returning to a fiery amber. Okay. She now knew that dark gold meant hotness, and bright amber meant anger. Well, if this was going to be more than a one-night fling, then at least, she'd always know where she stood with him. Not that she'd probably ever be around him again. And definitely not six months from now. Nope. Nu-uh.

"You're the perfect size, Maya. You've got a body just made for loving, and if you say that again, I'm gonna spank this lush ass of yours until it's shining red for me."

That should've made her cautious, but it didn't. Instead, her cunt tightened, silently screaming to be stuffed full of his cock, and spanked until she cried and begged for relief...in the form of an even harder fuck.

He tightened his hold on her rear, fingers digging into her ass cheeks. "Would you like to get spanked, Maya?"

She didn't answer him, but god, would she ever.

The man had to be stronger than an ox. Then again, he was a lion, one of the fiercest beasts in the world. Grrr.

Maya knew she was heavy, yet there he stood, supporting all of her weight as if she were nothing but a feather in the palm of his hand.

Biting her lip she finally nodded her answer to his question.

"Maybe after I take the edge off." Again, his eyes flashed a deep yellow. He was definitely turned-on.

Alex carried her a half-dozen steps through a door, and then dropped her in the middle of a bed. She didn't want to know why he had a bed in his office. Really, she didn't. And she definitely didn't want to know how many other women he'd banged on the very same mattress.

Maya lay sprawled before him, legs spread wide, showing off her well-loved pussy soaked in her cream, her breasts still bared from his mistreatment of her dress.

She should just have the word "slut" tattooed across her forehead.

She'd come to the club looking for action, but now, she had a hard time imagining being with anyone but Alex at the present. Not when he looked at her like she was the second coming of Aphrodite.

Maya watched, gaze transfixed, as her one-night lover began to strip before her eyes.

Alex whipped his near skin-tight shirt over his head and tossed it aside, revealing all of those lovely muscles she'd imagined beneath his clothes. God help her. His biceps were thick and heavily muscled, pecs were rock-hard, and those abs of his... She nearly moaned in delight at the beautiful sight of his perfectly sculpted stomach.

One, two, three...she kept counting the ripples until she stopped at eight. Then, there were those lovely lines at his hips that appeared to point down to the promise land. She wanted to lick and trace them with her tongue, follow them down beneath the cloth of his jeans.

His hands went to the button on his pants, readily gaining her full attention. She didn't spare a glance at his face. No, all she wanted right now was to see Mr. O'Connell's package. In a blink the pants were unsnapped, the zipper lowered. Good lord, the man wasn't wearing anything beneath the woven cotton.

That only made her prize easier to get to.

Alex nudged the waist of his jeans and they slid easily over his hips to fall to his ankles.

His dick... *Oh, damn...* His cock was long and thick, definitely looked as if he could fill her to the hilt, and then some. Pre-cum had already formed at the tip, and she wondered if the pearly drop of fluid would carry the same cinnamon-citrus flavor. She ached to lean forward and taste him.

He wrapped a hand around his shaft, stroked himself from root to tip and back again, repeating the gesture as she watched intently, forcing more of his seed to gather over his small slit. "See something you want, Maya?"

She nodded, not trusting herself to speak.

"Maybe after I've had you a few times."

She risked a glance at his face, and if he didn't look like he wanted to eat her alive, she'd demand a sample now. But those eyes were flickering between a fiery gold to nearly black, and it looked as if his face had more than the five o'clock shadow she'd seen earlier. Golden fur now peppered his cheeks.

Alex took a step toward her and stumbled, falling on top of her, and she let out a squeak in response to the sudden weight holding her down.

He, of course, growled. It seemed that her soon-to-be lover was a growler. She wanted to make him roar...

Giggling, she couldn't help but nudge him from her body, work at getting him to stand once again. "Alex? I think you forgot something," she stated, continuing to laugh.

He glared and cursed low before he crawled off of her, sitting back on the mattress to yank off his boots. She thought she heard him mutter something about mates asking for spankings.

Maybe he'd meant bedmates...

While he was busy with his clothing, she wiggled on the bed and yanked off the remnants of her dress, before reaching for her shoes. Of course, she didn't even get a chance to touch them.

A furry hand grasped her wrist and she stared into a pair of narrowed eyes. "The shoes stay."

He was looking more and more like his inner beast, the closer he came to fucking her. Oh, well. She supposed his well-defined muscles, along with his ridiculous hotness, could easily make up for a little extra body hair.

As for her, she was totally into a new category of slutiness—a fur loving slut. Hm... Did she still consider him to be just a one-night stand, or something else? Did she want him to be her lover? Perhaps, at least, lover-esque?

She wasn't sure. It didn't seem all that plausible that they'd get together past tonight. Why would they? No. Not even if her clit twitched and pulsed at the idea of spending more time with this lion, this hunky-as-hell Alex. But at the same time, she couldn't deny that this new acquaintance of hers was really getting under her skin...in the best of ways.

Now completely naked, her new lover turned his attention to her, shoving his way between her thighs, chasing her up to the head of the bed as she scrambled to keep up with him.

*

Alex's lion couldn't decide between diving back between her thighs for another taste or pushing his rock-hard cock into her silken heat, and claiming her as his.

Spread before him and still wearing her shoes, Maya was naked, showing him a sea of pale curves, and all he wanted to do was to lick and nibble every inch of her, discover her darkest secrets, and then ferret out even more, until he knew everything about her.

He palmed his cock, moved across the mattress on his knees, shifting their bodies until she was positioned exactly as he desired. Her golden-blonde hair spread across his pillows, his goddess rested against the soft surface of his bed, her knees bent and feet planted on the comforter, giving him a perfect view of her pretty, pink pussy.

Kneeling between her thighs Alex stared at this big, beautiful woman...his would-be mate.

'Cause yeah, the cat wanted her to be his, and after that first taste of her essence, the man in Alex wanted more too, and now, neither one of them were sure that a single night with Maya would ever be enough. Maybe after a hundred years or so, he thought, the two would have their fill. But not a minute sooner.

He squeezed his dick right below the head, teased the underside just below the crown. Damn, he couldn't wait for her to milk him, draw the cum out of his balls and deep into her waiting cunt.

Alex licked his lips, panting like a dog. The woman before him was a voluptuous, sensuous playground, and he couldn't wait for recess. The curve of her breasts, the dip of her waist and flare of her hips, called to him like no other woman's body ever had.

Which kinda made sense, since she was his true mate. Maya just didn't know it yet. She would, soon enough.

She kneaded her abundant breasts, plucked her nipples, and writhed beneath his gaze. All the while her attention remained focused on his hand stroking his cock.

"Temptress. Are you ready for me?"

Her small, pink tongue danced out to wet her lips, before disappearing again. He wanted to chase that enticing bit of muscle and search out more of her taste. This woman, his would-be mate, was a drug to both him and his lion.

She nodded, spread her thighs wider, showing him more of her moist pinkness. "Yes. Please?"

God, another growl built in his chest. The woman tested his control like no other.

Alex shifted his weight, leaned over her, and rested his bulk on one arm. Still gripping his shaft he rubbed the tip of his dick along her soaking slit, instantly shivering on contact.

"You're so hot for me, kitten." Yeah, his kitten. He barely recognized his own voice, and pretended that his beast wasn't stretching his skin thin, almost to the point of revealing itself. He knew fur had already sprouted over his body, his canines half-descended, and that the lion had taken over his voice.

Maya wrapped one of her thighs around his hip, pulling herself closer to him, scratching and clawing at his shoulders. "Need you...now."

"Soon..."

She whimpered and fell back onto the bed, hair fanning around her, exposing the delicate line of her neck, highlighting the smooth skin he couldn't wait to nibble...sink his teeth into, and mark her as his.

Alex kept up the slow, gentle rubbing of her pussy with the tip of his cock, gathering more and more of her cream with every pass of his dick along her swollen lower lips. Each time the head skimmed her hole, he had to fight his beast for control, resist the urge to slam right into her heat. No, he wanted to savor his first possession, at all cost. He wanted to tempt and tease her, before satisfying his own need.

Her pussy tried to suck him in, the flesh spasming and tightening, kissing the head of his cock, silently begging for him to enter. And each time he went near her silken entrance a shudder racked his body, shot along his spine and tugged at his balls. Fuck, he wasn't gonna last long. Not with her, his soon-to-be mate, and especially not during their first time.

With his next pass over her pussy he paused, inched his dick in, and let her cunt suckle the head of his cock. Fuck. The hot, wet heat cradled him, massaged him, causing him to bare his teeth. Growling and panting a hiss left his mouth before he could bite it back.

Maya flexed her legs, as if trying to force his entry, but he was a lion, the pride's prime. Head lion in charge. No way would she be able to move him along, hurry his pace.

With a gentle shift he let his crown retreat, and then slide inside her once again, equally teasing them both with his barely-there penetration.

"Damn it, Alex." She tightened her thighs again, and had the nerve to growl at him, bare her teeth. Shit, that was hot.

"When I'm ready, sweet." He took great care while he lowered his body over hers, the muscles of his arms straining to be gentle with his human mate. He swept down, captured her lips and slipped his tongue into her mouth, fucked the moist cavern in the same rhythm as his cock toyed with her pussy.

He rolled his hips, slow and easy, giving her just another inch, a slightly deeper penetration, but still withheld his entire shaft from going all the way in. He wanted her to beg, to cry with need, to be willing to accede to anything he demanded.

Like...becoming his mate.

Or, at least, just agreeing to be his.

He could always work on the "mate" thing later.

The damned beast was riding him hard, snarling and snapping and demanding that Alex let it take control, let it sink its canines into his mate and claim her. Like, right now.

Maya moaned into his mouth as she fought for dominance, making his lion puff with pride at the fact that its mate could hold her own against him, giving as well as she took. Alex pulled away from her inviting mouth in increments, slowed and calmed their fight until their lips were barely a hairsbreadth apart, forcing them to share each other's breath.

"Please, I need you."

He couldn't hide the smile that took over his lips. "How bad?"

"It hurts. So bad." She leaned up, nipped his lower lip.

Alex then rained gentle kisses along her jaw, and was pleased when she tilted her head to the side, granting him better access, subconsciously submitting to him. He licked and nibbled a path to her ear, caught the lobe between his teeth.

"Are you mine, sweet Maya?" He bit the spot below her ear, reveled in her quick, indrawn breath, the shudder that traveled through her, causing her sweet cunt to tighten around his shallow invasion.

"Yesss."

"You belong to me, don't you?" Alex laved at the spot again, and traveled farther south along the column of her neck.

"God, yes."

The cat was pleased, and her admission helped to ease the painful scratching and clawing that came from inside his body. "I'm going to keep you, and this sweet, luscious body in my bed, and I'm not gonna let you go." She nodded against him, but he wanted to hear the words. "Say it, sweet Maya. Tell me you agree."

"Fuck. Yes. You're keeping me in your bed."

Prickles of pain came from inside his mouth, and Alex knew the beast wouldn't be denied any longer. He opened his jaws, placed his teeth against the soft, tender skin of her shoulder, and sank his sharp canines into her flesh. At that exact moment he shoved his cock deep into her pussy, sheathing himself to the hilt. Maya arched into him, head tilted back and gritting her teeth. A soft whimper escaped her lips.

A growl formed in his chest and the lion snarled and roared, reveled in the taste of its mate's blood sliding over his tongue. He drank down the fluid, and let his saliva slip into her body to mingle with her blood stream.

Then the man emerged... Alex froze, fully seated in her cunt, a bolt of pleasure overtaking him with each tremor that traveled through her silken heat.

Distantly, he heard a shout of pleasure. Maya clutched at his shoulders, legs firm and strong around his waist, and she tilted her hips, as if she longed for deeper penetration.

"Alex, Alex, Alex..." She chanted his name, and so, he picked up the rhythm, timed the flexing of his hips, the thrust and retreat of his cock to punctuate her words.

With her claimed, and the transition beginning in her body at the DNA level, Alex was free to take her as he desired. He gently withdrew his teeth from her shoulder and lapped at the wound to start the healing process, and all the while he kept his hips moving, pistoning his cock in and out of her sweet cunt.

Wound now taken care of he turned his attention to pleasing her, his true mate. Alex pushed himself up so he could stare into her eyes, watch her as her pleasure unfolded.

Maya released her hold on his hips, dropped her feet to the mattress, and began meeting each of his thrusts, the sound of flesh on flesh filling the room, mingling with the heavy panting of their ragged breathing.

He kept up his tempo, hard slams of his cock into her quivering pussy, her heat milking and massaging his shaft. "Fuck, Maya. You have such a perfect little cunt."

That earned him a tight squeeze of his dick, her mouth opening on a gasp.

"You like that, don't you? Like hearing how much I love fucking this pussy?" Her slippery sheath rippled. "I want you to come on my dick. Then, I'll come deep inside you." Her walls gripped him tight, eyes glazed with passion.

Fuck, just watching her got him nice and close to coming. His balls drew up tight against him, aching to let go, fill her pussy up with his cum.

Observing her reaction he increased his pace, angled his hips until he got the response he was waiting for. A tilt, a swivel, and then...

Her entire body trembled, eyes fluttering shut as Maya cried out, "Alex!"

And there it was. He'd found the sweet spot inside his mate once again. In time he knew he'd be able to find her G-spot without a problem, and he'd enjoy every minute of learning exactly how to pleasure her.

With every thrust their pelvises met, pressing against her clit while his dick stroked against her happy place inside. Each entrance was greeted with a tightening of her pussy, a tantalizing rhythm that seemed to be begging for his cum.

He was panting with effort, sweat coating his back and brow as he tried his best to please her. His beast was totally onboard with that plan, wanted to make sure its mate was fully satisfied.

Her short fingernails dug into the skin of his arms and shoulders, pushing his arousal higher, lion and man both loving the fierceness of their mate. Alex wanted more of her marks, wanted her to scar him, as he'd just scarred her. He couldn't take her bite just yet, not with her transition still incomplete, but the scratches and gouges would do for now.

The rhythmic tremor of her pussy increased, coming faster and faster, milking him harder than before.

"That's it, sweet. Come for me..." Alex panted the words, the effort to hold back his own orgasm increasing with every thrust of his cock inside her slick pussy.

She tossed her head back and forth, babbling, sobbing, and begging all at once. Her petite hands released his shoulders and moved to fondle her breasts, fingertips playing over her nipples, and he'd be lying if he didn't ache for another taste. "Give me one of your tits, Maya. Show me how much you want my mouth."

"Fuck, Alex..." She did as he asked, holding it steady for him while he lowered his head.

He pulled the nipple into his mouth, every suck mimicked by a tightening of her pussy as if the two were connected. She dug her nails into his scalp and the lion roared inside him, rejoiced in its mate taking what she needed, shoving her breast farther into his mouth.

Alex nibbled, bit and teased her, hoping to yank her orgasm closer with his every move. He expected her to explode for him at any moment, her breath increasing with each slide of his cock, his mouth and teeth on her nipple, lightly grazing the sensitive nub.

"G-Gonna..."

He released her breast, captured her gaze with his. "Do it, Maya. Come on my dick."

Beneath his focus, she came apart. Her eyes widened, back arched and mouth dropped open on a scream. That sweet, wet pussy clamped tight around him, and his dick responded in kind, throbbing and twitching in her canal, balls high and tight and ready to shoot his cum.

Her orgasm seemed to go on and on and he still worked to keep his pace, drawing out her pleasure while taking his own.

With a shift of his hands he grasped her unbitten shoulder, held her steady while he prepared to force another orgasm from her. His body was ready to come deep inside her, with his pleasure gathering by the moment, each ragged breath drawing his climax closer.

He increased the speed and strength of his strokes, her pussy still responding to his fucking. The slaps of their bodies turned into fierce slams, his sweet mate passionately meeting each thrust, compelling him to increase the power behind his moves.

"Fuck yeah. Take it, Maya."

"Yes, yes, yes..."

His balls smacked against the bottoms of her ass while he pounded into her, and he could feel his climax right there, teetering on the very edge. The pleasure, the ecstasy of being inside his mate, rose with each second, hurtling him over his own precipice.

"Come inside me, Alex!"

Alex couldn't quiet his lion's growl if he wanted to, the animal taking control, as if he were trying to somehow pleasure Maya even more.

"Gonna...come!"

"God, yes."

His fulfillment was in reach, and the beast propelled him over the edge. His balls emptied inside her, filled her soaking pussy with his cum, body trembling and spasming with the force of his overdue orgasm. Breathing took a backseat to the ecstasy he felt, the joy of stuffing his mate with his seed, painting her inner walls while rolling in utter bliss. He bucked and jerked, cock mimicking his body's motions while he came, pulsing deep inside her sweet little hole. His hips kept moving, but without any rhythm, spurred on by his orgasm, with pleasure overtaking his every move.

With Alex's hips still sealed to his mate's, he felt the tremors ease and slow in time, as did his breathing, until he simply lay panting over her, his body resting and aligning with her abundant curves, cushioning him with her warmth.

"Mm..." Maya sounded sated, happy.

His cat was damned cocky about that fact.

Turning his head he lapped at the nearly-healed bite, pink scars the only reminders of his claiming.

Maybe she wouldn't notice until he had a moment to explain. Maybe he'd get a year leeway or something. Wishful thinking.

Holding tight he rolled them until his lazing mate covered him like a blanket, his cock still comfortably resting in her pussy. She squeaked at his move, but quickly settled, and buried her face in his neck.

Alex stroked her back, soothed and petted her, his lion finally at ease, now that its mate was fully claimed. The damned thing was purring.

"That was," she breathed against his neck, snuggled closer, "amazing."

"Mm-hm." He was afraid to say anything else, not quite sure how he was going to explain his earlier actions. His beast had finally relinquished control, teeth and hair receding, until Alex was pretty sure he looked human once again.

He slid his hands farther south, kneaded and squeezed her ass, enjoyed the feel of her heavy globes in his palms. She was made for him, plump and soft in all the right places. The perfect woman to carry his cubs, to nurture them, to mother them. *Purrfect.*

"Thank you." She shifted, pushed up as if to leave him.

Never! He shifted his hold, and wrapped his arms around her shoulders. "You said you were mine, sweet." He worked very, very hard at not sounding psychotically possessive.

"I... But... That was just..."

"That was just me saying you're not going to leave my bed. Ever." Okay, he was totally being psychotically possessive.

She fought his grasp, and he eased his hold a little, letting her raise her chest, but still keeping a firm grip on her waist. "Look. This was fun, but—"

Alex placed a finger over her lips. "But you loved every minute, no? Tell me you're not attracted to me. Tell me this doesn't feel really right, and that you truly want to walk out that door and never see me again."

He already knew her answer even if she didn't want to face the truth. That she yearned to be near him as much as his lion demanded that she always be close at hand.

She shook her head. "Alex..."

He sighed. "How about you just stay the night? Let me make breakfast for you in the morning?"

Maya relaxed against him once again. "This is totally against one-night stand etiquette, you know. You're supposed to kick me out now."

Alex laughed. Because, whether she knew it or not, Maya wasn't leaving him. Ever.

Chapter Three

Tiptoe through the window...

Okay, she wasn't going to be tiptoeing anywhere. It'd be more like cautiously creeping, with carefully plotted movements. Plus, she wasn't headed out of a window, because there weren't any.

Maya's whole body hurt, but in a very good, and never bad, gimme more kinda way. Wow. Alex could seriously fuck a girl stupid. Three times when it was all said and done. She'd never been with a guy with that kind of stamina, and he woulda given her more if she hadn't told him he'd broken her vagina. But then again, Alex wasn't your ordinary man.

Seriously.

Of course, after he'd "broken" it, he had to apologize, going down on her once more before letting her pass out from being fucked senseless.

Not that she was complaining.

She was totally going to have to get with Gina before the next kitty orgy. And by then, maybe Alex could be two-night material.

Yum.

Maya inched toward her edge of the bed, eyes and attention focused on the hot hunk of cat-man next to her. She was surprised when he didn't move as she extricated herself from the bed. In two shakes she rolled her naked self from the mattress, landing not-so-eloquently with a soft thump. As quick as a fluffy rabbit she popped her head back up and breathed a sigh of relief when she saw that he was still asleep. Aw, Alex looked so cute, pillow cuddled to his chest and nose buried in the plush fabric.

Okay, enough. She had to get a move on. Distant sounds of people stirring down in the club filtered up the stairs and to her ears, which to her, meant she should truck on out of bow-chicka-bow-bow land, and back into her real world. She just needed to get through her walk of shame, and then, she'd be home free.

Watching Alex she carefully padded through his room and removed a club shirt from his closet. A quick peek into his dresser netted her a pair of sweatpants. Damn, she prayed they'd fit.

Walk of shame outfit hastily chosen she slipped the "borrowed" garments on, then snagged her shoes and purse. She didn't bother trying to hunt up the remnants of her dress or panties. Without a doubt, they were a lost cause.

She moved ever-so-quiet as a mouse through the room...

Heh. Mouse. And he was a cat. She nearly snorted. Maya made it to the office door and slipped back into the main club with Alex being none the wiser.

Score one for Maya!

Feeling oddly triumphant she stood on the main floor with a solitary destination in mind. Front door to the rescue!

Except...

Except two strong arms grabbed her from behind, wrapped around her waist and tugged her back against a tall, firm body, a hard cock nestled along the crack of her ass.

But it wasn't Alex. She twitched her nose...oh, no, he didn't... He didn't smell like Alex, and there was no hint of the man she'd spent the night with surrounding her. A part of her bristled at a stranger touching her.

Maya twisted, tried to free her arms from the ones holding her captive, and her defiance was met with a low growl, the deep, penetrating sound reverberating through her. "Hold still, baby. I'm aching for another go. One for the road."

The stranger leaned forward, nuzzled her neck much like Alex had done last night, but it didn't have that same tender feeling. It seriously squicked her out.

The guy reached up and palmed her breast, the shirt she wore the only thing keeping him from touching her skin. God, revulsion poured through her, the mere idea of someone besides Alex reaching beneath the shirt, getting skin-to-skin with her, was enough to have her go all badass ninja on his ass. "Let go of me!"

"A fighter. Ooh, yeah, babe. I see you want it a little rough. Sure, I can do that." He nosed her hair out of the way, took a deep breath against her skin. By now, she figured it was a shifter thing. They seemed to rely on their senses a lot.

Icky guy behind her froze the moment he'd taken a full breath, and then let it out with a heavy gust, dropping his arms in a split-second, instantly leaving her personal space. "I-I'm s-sorry. Didn't mean...didn't know... You'll tell him, right? That I had no idea?"

Maya turned to face the guy, with a fierce, uncontrollable anger pouring through her veins. He wasn't unattractive or anything. No, in a strictly clinical sense, she could appreciate his muscle-packed body and strong bone structure. He just didn't do it for her. Not like Alex. Really who could, after their passion-filled night?

She sighed. She figured she'd probably be hung up on the man upstairs for a while. Argh. Stupid hot hottie. Why did he have to affect her so?

The guy stumbled back even farther away from her, tripping over a chair in his haste to put more space between them. "Right? You'll tell him?"

Damn, she couldn't ignore his constant pleading, or the sheer look of fright on his face. Maybe it was a cat thing? That guys didn't do women who'd just spent the night with another? She nodded. "Sure, I'll tell him."

He ran a hand through his hair. "Okay. Good. Thanks." He heaved out a breath. "Right. Do you need any help, Prima?" *Prima?* Maybe this was another shifter thing? "Have you eaten? I-I could make you some breakfast, if you'd like. If you can find a place to sit." He gestured toward the rest of the club, and Maya took a good look at her surroundings.

Dang, the place had been destroyed! She now noticed at least a dozen naked bodies all piled together across the room. Apparently, cats took their orgies pretty damn seriously.

"Um, no. I'm just gonna go home. And, uh..."

"Prime okayed it?"

Shifters. She had to remind herself she was around an entirely different species, one that had their own set of rules and whatnot. "You mean Alex? Sure. We're good." She nodded to emphasize the point, and prayed that he couldn't smell a lie or anything.

"Oh, okay. Right this way." Thank goodness he believed her.

Mr. No-Longer-Creepy-Guy helped her navigate safely through the bodies, and she even managed to not step on anyone's extremities. With a nervous smile the guy disengaged the alarm and unlocked the door, holding it wide and waiting for her to exit.

"Did Prime assign you any guards?"

Dude. One-night stands got guards? Wow. Had to be a totally weird shifter thing. "Uh, no, I'm a big girl. Besides, I know Tae Bo. I'll be fine."

The man didn't look completely convinced. His eyebrows furrowed, but Maya didn't give him the time to stop her, she just glided through the doorway with a quick wave, and scurried through the parking lot to her car like she was walking barefoot on hot coals. It was Saturday, and she had things to do. Like, going home, getting cleaned up, and then heading to the grocery store.

She was hella hungry for some steaks. As in plural.

So, it'd be to the grocery store first.

Once in her car she started up her little putter-putter deathtrap and popped it into gear. The tiny box of hell—as her mother called it—was a sporty 1976 Fiat Spider. Being a semi-cute fluffy chick, she thought that she should have a car that would ratchet her right up to "full-cute." At least, in her mind.

Plus, it pissed off her strict family. Bonus!

At the edge of the parking lot, Maya checked for oncoming cars, then carefully pulled out into the early morning traffic.

Between the roar of her engine and the wind whipping at her face, she couldn't hear much, but she coulda sworn that a distant roar came from the direction of the club.

Huh.

*

Alex would not hurt one of his own cats. No. And he wouldn't permanently scar the man for simply sniffing his mate. Or tear his arms and legs off for touching her. Or kill him because he'd sent the pride's new prima alone into the world and without a guard, while she was undergoing the change.

He took a deep, cleansing breath, and then another and yet another. The lion kneeling before him, Jenner, professed he hadn't known that the woman was mated to Alex, and that Maya hadn't yet been introduced to the pride.

The lion still wanted to do him bodily harm. But he restrained himself.

Jenner also pleaded that he was late to scent the mating mark, because the entire club was drenched in sex.

The lion in Alex wanted Jenner for dinner. Not really, but the lion was definitively furious. Maybe he would just chase him for a bit, play like he was a predator hunting his prey, you know, and scare the ever-living-crap out of him.

Alex clenched his fists, releasing the tension and tightening it once again, while he fought with his inner beast. He knew without looking that his face had elongated, forming into a snout, fur sprouting along his arms and cheeks, his fingers turning into claws.

The cat was *pissed*.

"Where did she say she was going?" He ignored the fact that he sounded more lion than man.

"Home maybe? I think." The younger lion swallowed, and the cat in Alex instinctively followed the bob of the man's Adam's apple, imagining his teeth ripping Jenner's throat out.

Okay, so he was edgy. No, he was much, much beyond edgy.

"Grayson!" He watched his second crawl from beneath a pile of bodies, nudging both women and men sprawled on top of him. Naked as the day he was born, his second approached.

It didn't take the man more than two steps to realize Alex was ready to lose all control. Grayson immediately dropped his gaze, his expression assuming a mantle of submission as he approached.

"Prime."

Alex grunted. "Bring me Gina, and find out anything you can about a Maya Josephs that lives in the area. Address. Phone number. Family. Everything. Anything." Grayson didn't move fast enough for him, and so, he snarled, "*Now*."

His second scampered away. Were it any other time he might've found humor in the way the large lion ran, but right now, he was seriously P.O.'ed that the man wasn't running fast enough.

Alex paced while he waited, anxiously striding back and forth in front of the bar, nudging and shoving body parts out of his way as he moved. His cats and familiar humans scattered and whimpered, sensing his foul mood.

He knew the pride could feel his tension. The anger and unrest pouring through him in waves had to undoubtedly unsettle them. He stopped just long enough to roll his shoulders and crack his neck. Alex had not awoken a happy kitty. Far from it. He'd *expected* to rise with his mate in his arms. He'd *expected* her to be hot and ready for him to take her again. He'd *expected* to feed and nourish her through her change, until a gorgeous lioness stood before him.

What he'd gotten was the opposite. An empty bed with his mate gone, and to make things worse, Maya, lovely Maya, had been accosted by one of his lions. And then...she escaped, back into her world. And he didn't like it one bit.

Shit, fuck, damn, and growl.

After some time, too long for his agitated state, Gina stood before him, completely nude and looking rather weary from sex.

"You're standing there like you're the cat that ate the cream."

Alex approached, the weight of his lion filling each of his steps, his predatory beast barely caged beneath his skin. He stepped in front of her, inches separating their bare bodies. He'd been so torn over Maya's absence that he hadn't bothered to dress.

"Gina."

"*Alex*..." The bitch had the audacity to purr and reach for him.

He could feel the movement of a lion from behind, probably warning the woman of his irritable mood.

Alex captured Gina's wrist, squeezed and tightened his hold until she realized her serious predicament. "Jenner, if you want to keep all of your limbs intact, you'll stop dancing behind me like a treat for my beast."

A squeak was his only response. It was funny how one of his strongest lions could become cub-like in two-seconds-flat, merely at his cat's displeasure.

Alex turned his attention back to the woman before him, squeezing harder and harder as the seconds passed. When Gina finally whimpered and dropped her gaze, he figured she'd gotten his point.

"P-Prime." The word was barely a whisper, but it was at least, said with respect.

"You've caused a problem, Gina. You let an unknown female into Genesis, for the Gaian Moon. You risked not only the human's safety, but you also risked the pride's secrets from getting out. And to think...it was all out of spite." He spit the words out, each one tasting fouler than the one before. Regardless whether or not there were consequences to her actions, Gina had still violated their laws. "Though we have few laws and few secrets, your selfish actions still threatened both pride and shifters alike." Alex didn't think it possible, but the normally proud and haughty female shrunk even smaller before his eyes. Murmurs surrounded him, but he didn't take his focus from the she-cat. "Your fate will be decided at a later date. For now, you'll work with Grayson to find the female, and then, you'll be restricted to the confines of your home."

Gina gasped, her frightful gaze flashing to his. "But, Prime..."

Alex again tightened his hold, felt the rub of bone-on-bone. "Silence. You won't lose any of your *little toys* while under house arrest. You'll speak to your employer...use up some of your vacation time that you have saved up. Now, go help my second before I drop you where you stand."

The entire room fell silent at his pronouncement, and neither lion nor human in the room dared to breathe, until he released his hold on Gina's wrist and she scrambled away from him.

He knew he would later regret being so harsh... But right now, his anger and frustration got the better of him. His conscience would have to wait though, after he'd secured his mate in his den and ensured her safety. Which sure as hell needed to be sooner rather than later. The last thing Ridgeville needed was a she-cat prowling around, having no training on how to control her hunger, her inner beast. Or her shift.

Shit, fuck, damn, and growl.

Chapter Four

Owie, owie, owie...

God, Maya must've burned like, a gazillion calories, while doing the horizontal mambo with Alex. Seriously. She'd never been so sore or hungry in her life—like the hunger inside her was a living, breathing thing, furiously trying to gnaw its way out of her empty stomach in search of food.

Couple that with an uncharacteristic royal bitch attitude, and she was batting a thousand. It felt like she'd suddenly become schizophrenic, and had another personality to deal with inside her head. One that was very, very cranky.

At the grocery store, she snagged a cart and went directly to the meat department. No other aisle for now. *Do not pass go.* Go right past the delicious bakery, and head straight to the meat section. Cranky or not, hungry or not, there would be no eating of the people who got in her way. Because, really, that seemed like a pretty good idea, her empty stomach thought.

Reaching the back section of the store, she stared at the plethora of beef before her. And it had to be beef. Because chicken, fish, and pork, just weren't gonna cut it. Part of her balked at her sudden, insatiable craving for meat, but the other part, the stronger part that seemed to be prowling, dragging its nails inside her brain, told her to grab it all and eat it raw, bathe in the blood to feed her hunger.

Okay, ew, just yuck.

Maya had no problem purchasing pounds upon pounds of meat. Besides, Atkins involved the whole low carb thing, and it'd been a minute since she'd gone on a diet. So yeah, she was game, but she sure as hell wasn't eating it raw, though.

Nu-uh.

The weird "prowly thing" in her head snarled a little, but finally gave in. She really should've had Alex let her sleep a little. And while she was at it, he should've told her that sex with him came with a second personality.

Her resolve to quell her hunger firmly in place, she snatched up a few steaks. Then a few more. And a dozen pounds or so of ground beef for good measure. Fatty good stuff. Atkins was about low carbs, not low fat content.

Maya growled at anyone that got too close. Her food. All hers!

A familiar sound reached her ears—the padding of quick feet, the loud squeaking of shoes on shiny floors, gave her friend's approach away. Maya swiveled her head and narrowed her eyes. Carly was her friend, but...would she try to take her food...?

"Maya?" The woman's face was easy to read, happy, not predatory in the least bit.

Okay then. She took a deep breath, scented the air, and something teased her nostrils. Something wild and sweet, and it made her slightly...hungrier, believe it or not. The prowling presence within stretched and scratched inside her head, snarled yet again. Maya decided she had to be going crazy. Certifiable. Because she suddenly had the urge to eat her friend. And not in a good way. No, she wanted her friend for lunch.

Maya licked her lips, nose flaring with each step closer that the slim woman took. Yum. "Grrr."

"M-Maya?" Carly stopped, and with four feet separating them, Maya could hear the rapid thumping of the woman's heart, her forced breathing.

Her friend was scared. Of her?

Hm...scared made hunting the prey all the better, she thought. Yummy.

Wait! That thought, the idea of her friend as some sort of prey, snapped Maya's attention back to reality, and away from that freaky, homicidal part of her brain.

"Oh, shit." Maya slapped a hand over her mouth and ran straight for the bathroom, bile rising in her throat.

God, she ran faster than she'd ever run before. As if she had wings Maya flew by the other customers, weaving and dodging little old ladies in panic until she burst through the bathroom, and then through a stall door, bending over a toilet as she tried to calm the sickly feeling in her stomach. Wave after wave of retching crashed her insides, over and over as she fought for breath, fought to keep her composure.

A soft hand stroked her back, announcing to Maya that her friend was there to comfort her. Carly's scent discerned Maya blindly reached for the paper towel her friend offered. She then wiped her face before standing to face the other woman.

"Carly... I'm..."

How in the world was she supposed to explain her actions? To tell her friend that she was ready to hurl because...? Because she looked good enough to eat? Like, literally.

"Shh... It's okay. Everything's going to be okay." She rubbed Maya's shoulders and pulled her close, then wrapped an arm around her waist and led her toward the bathroom door. "Let's go back and get your meat, and then we can go to my house, okay? I'll have my brother come over to talk you through this, honey."

"Your brother? Why? What are you talking—?"

"Don't worry. You'll understand, soon enough. I promise."

Maya and Carly hugged, a soft whimper sounding in her throat. God, she wasn't sure what was happening to her, like why she suddenly had such a craving for meat, or why she even thought that her friend seemed to be a good choice for lunch. Maya wondered if she needed an antipsychotic, or something just as strong...

Once they reentered the store various scents assaulted her senses. As the smell of raw meat tempted her, called to her, she could hear the heartbeat of every passing shopper. And they all looked so delicious, reminded that growly-prowly sensation in her mind, seemingly interested in several of the individuals perusing the produce section. Maya licked her lips and swallowed the pooling saliva in her mouth. Yeah, she supposed that *interested* could be one way to describing the feelings she had. *Ravenous* was yet another.

"Carly, there's something really, really wrong with me. Like, really." She knew she hadn't just woken up this morning, and decided, "Hey, let's be a cannibal today. Yay!"

"I know." Her friend kept a comforting arm around her shoulders, a tight grip on her other hand. "Let's go and see Andrew, okay?"

With Carly leading the way, they approached a slim man with fluffy hair, wearing wire-rimmed glasses that graced his oval-shaped face. He was adorable in a twitchy, I'd-rather-not-be-your-next-dinner, kind of way.

"Hey, Andrew." The guy jerked and took a step away from them, but Carly held out a hand to halt his backward progress. "We've got a situation."

The guy then eyed Maya, and she had the sudden urge to growl and hiss at him. The guy was staring, damn it. She'd show him his place.

"W-What kind of a situation?"

Carly stroked her, released her long enough to run a hand down her hair, and Maya leaned in to her friend's soothing touch.

"It looks like we've got a *Carni 3S*. Can you give me a day's worth of meat at the local price? I'll pull around back."

"*3S?*" She practically purred, her friend's touch still calming her.

"Um... That stands for Sudden Something Situation. Get it?"

She only half listened, because Andrew swallowed, and just like that, she was filled with the desire to snack on him. The guy wouldn't miss a chunk or two, right? She licked her lips and took a step forward, only to be halted by her friend, and she snarled in response, jerked against Carly. Just a little nibble?

"Maya, no. Bad doggie."

Dog? She wasn't a dog! She snarled again, snapped her teeth and hissed. A split-second after the sound had left her mouth, she covered her lips and gasped. "Oh, god. Carly, what's wrong with me?" She whimpered.

"What'd you do last night, M? Hm?" The other woman stroked her head and she leaned in to the caress. The mean, hungry *thing* in her head calmed a bit, still aching for meat, but satisfied for the moment by the gentle touch.

"I went out." She nuzzled the small hand. "Genesis had this...this thing last night." She seriously wasn't telling her friend, especially in front of a complete stranger, that she'd gone to a shifter orgy. No fucking way. "Spent some time with the owner. No biggie."

Carly froze, and Maya growled until the brushing motion picked up again. "Okay. Okay, we can deal with this. Andrew? Meat. Now." Through heavy-lidded eyes she watched the man scamper away, and the bitch inside her wanted to pounce on him. She jerked, ready to chase, but Carly held her firm. "No. Let's go get in the car, and we'll go over to Ian's. You remember Ian, right?"

She nodded. Okay, yeah...why not? Ian was a hottie, she could certainly go over there... As long as she had meat to eat.

"Good girl." Carly kept petting her as they walked, as they shuffled toward the front of the building and into her friend's car. "We'll deal with your car later."

Good girl? Hm... Maya was a good little freak of nature. Mostly. She only tried to eat, like five people, right? But she didn't.

Maybe she'd turned into a zombie.

A very hungry, cranky, and tired zombie.

To top it off...she missed Alex.

Damn it. What in the world was happening to her?

* * *

Grayson and Gina hadn't had to look very far to find Maya. One phone call to his second, from Carly's brother Ian, was all it took for Gina to come off of his shit list. For now.

Alex needed to remember that he shouldn't kill the man standing before him. Ian, the lead buck of Thompson Warren was a good man, a good rabbit, and had helped his mate in her time of need.

But he'd also put his hands on Maya.

For good reason, he reminded himself. Ian understood the necessity, of Maya being in the middle of her transition, of needing a strong, steel cage to hold her captive, until Alex arrived.

Still, his lion wanted to eat the rabbit for dinner. A loud, snarling roar echoed up the stairs, and he winced at the troubling sound. Damn it to hell, his mate was not a happy she-cat.

Then again, the rabbits facing him weren't happy, either. Both Ian and his sister Carly, glared at him as he stood on the porch. As much as a rabbit could glare at a lion.

Carly pounced first. "You turned her, Alex." She stepped forward and poked him in the chest and he took it, overcome with the knowledge that he probably deserved every culpable word she threw his way. "She has no idea about us, other than what we've revealed to the general populace. You let her into Genesis during your *fuck-like-bunnies* moon. How dare you?"

"Now, Miss Thomp—"

Carly growled, little pink nose twitching. If he wasn't mated and devoted to Maya, he'd likely find it to be cute.

"Shut it." She punched him in the chest and he flinched. "You knew what could happen to an unfamiliar human in your den during the moon, and you not only let her stay, but you bit her, *and* get mated. Argh!"

Alex frowned. "I understand your concerns." He then sighed, ran a hand through his hair. "It wasn't my intention to let her go this morning, but one of my pride—"

The small rabbit bristled, and he imagined that if she were shifted, her rabbit hair would be all puffed-up in anger.

He wasn't going to smile at the image.

He just wasn't.

"Let her go? *Let her go?*" She bared her little white teeth at him, which kinda reminded him of Chiclets, and then spun on her heel, curses trailing behind her as she stomped away from him. "You deal with the lion, Ian. I swear I'll gnaw through his jugular if I have to talk to him another second! Rabbits can be carnivores, too!"

Alex watched as Carly plodded in anger, then turned his attention to the buck. "I'm sorry if I, or my mate, have caused your warren any undue stress. If you'll just take me to where you're keeping her..." He let the sentence trail off, to see what type of response he'd receive.

Ian huffed out a breath, not unlike a frustrated sigh, and dropped his shoulders. "You couldn't have picked anyone other than my sister's best friend? Really?"

Normally, the leaders of the various shifter clans got along well, and they tried not to cause any unnecessary trouble amongst themselves. It seemed that turning Maya, his little she-cat, had caused a fuck-ton of grief. For everyone involved.

Ian began, "Well, what's done is done, I suppose. I'll try to talk my sister's anger down to a manageable level. I'm sure once she's had time to think—" A loud, thundering crash, followed by a spine-shivering scraping of metal-on-metal, echoed from the basement. "Fuck!" Ian spun and ran toward the commotion, feet pounding on the solid wood floor, with Alex following closely on the buck's heels.

The deeper into the house they traveled the louder the roars became, until Maya's hisses and growls surrounded them...

His she-cat's sounds of anger were echoed by another, but lower, softer one.

"Oh, shit." Alex recognized it. He'd chased his share of natural rabbits through the forest to know that his mate was about to make her best friend—dinner.

Ian dove for the closed door, but Alex got there first. Pulling the man out of the way, he said, "I'll get her, Buck. I'll take care of this. The last thing you want to be is Maya's next course."

The leader of the rabbits narrowed his eyes at him as he took a step back. "Calm her, and get my sister out alive, Prime, or—"

Alex didn't have the time to argue with the man, nor did he have the time to remind the rabbit about who was who on the food chain. With a quick nod Alex turned, yanked open the basement door, and delved into something he could only describe as a "furry" hell.

A dim light enveloped him as he stormed in, shedding his shirt and undoing his belt as fast as his hands allowed. Partially into his shift his arrival did nothing to distract his mate. Not when the scent of fresh meat clouded the air. No, Maya' focus rested solely on the far corner of the room. Undoubtedly where her rabbit friend hid for her life.

Alex's lion clawed at him, hungry for both its mate and the tempting scent of raw meat that filled the air.

Another high-pitched hiss sounded. Alex tried, "Maya!"

She glanced at him, but returned her attention to her unfortunate prey.

"Mate!" He allowed some of his beast to filter into his voice, into his command. When Maya swung her head around and glared at him for the second time, it was with bared teeth and a fierce snarl. "Come on, baby. It's me." He circled the room, watched as she trailed him, following his every movement with her fiery gaze. He toed off his boots and unsnapped his jeans, exposed more of his body.

She'd either attack and he'd have to go "furry" to pin her, or she'd shift back and pounce on him in human form. God, untimely as it might be, he was really hoping for the latter.

Focus now squarely on him Maya licked her chops, her gaze curiously intent on what he revealed. "Hey, sweetheart. I'm sorry about this morning, about what's happening—" Alex didn't finish the sentence, didn't know how to explain himself at this very moment. He'd been a selfish prick, but for good reason. Maya and he belonged together. "I-I couldn't help myself. Please...let me make it up to you. You, my mate, shouldn't have had to deal with this alone." He inched his pants down a little farther, let his dick pop free.

He was turned-on by his mate's fierce display, and he wanted nothing more than to take her. Right here, right now. Fuck, his dick was rock-hard, long and thick before him, and more than ready to claim the beauty crouching merely a few feet away.

Alex stroked his dick, smiled when she snarled, her focus fixed on his cock. "Shift for me, mate, and let me feed your hunger." She snarled again, but didn't approach, her attention flicking between his groin and his face. "You are my mate, sweet Maya, and all you need to do is slip back into your human skin for me, and I'll prove it to you."

A blur of white to his right snagged both of their attention, but Alex reactively snapped his fingers to reclaim Maya's concentration. "You don't want that, baby. I've got what you need. Right here."

Maya growled and stepped closer, closing the short distance between them. Alex reached out to her, ran his fingers through her golden fur as soon as she was within range. "That's a sweet mate. She-cat, you need to let Maya back out to play. Let her claim her mate, and then we can find our fur together."

The lioness huffed, but then sat back on her haunches and closed her eyes. *Thank god.*

In moments the distinct sounds of popping bones, as her body reshaped and returned to her human state, filled the room. Alex winced at each and every noise that spoke of her transformation, knowing that her first few shifts would often be painful and tiring. He really was a selfish prick, wasn't he?

Seconds ticked past as golden fur receded, her face reshaping to its previous form, her body becoming a study in curves that he would forever remember. Alex crouched down, careful not to touch her until the change was complete. The last thing he needed was for her to snap back into her animal state to claw the shit out of him.

Before long she lay naked on the carpet, breathing heavy as she found herself. Inhaling deep she raised her attention to him, and he smiled, preparing for the meeting of their gazes. Sure, he'd gone about things in an ass-backwards kind of a way, but he could only hope that once he had the chance to explain himself, that Maya and her she-cat would reciprocate the feelings that he and his lion had for them. And then, things should fall into place…and it should all go smoothly…

"You ass-sniffing, butt-crack licking, litter box-using fuckhole!"

Or not.

Chapter Five

Maya panted and heaved as she lay sprawled on her best friend's basement floor, staring at the cause for her personal hell with blood boiling through her veins.

"Now, Maya..." He held out his hands as if to placate her. Fuck that. Fuck him.

She pushed to her knees, and then to her feet, pain slowly receding as the seconds passed. "*Do not* 'Now, Maya' me."

Feeling more herself again, she stood tall and filtered through the mixed emotions coursing through her body. Of course, the human half of her brain, because there were two sides now—woohoo!—was pissed as all get out, and ready to go crouching lioness on his stupid ass. Regardless of how hot he was. But the feline whore within was all about rubbing her furry body on the gorgeous man.

Traitor.

Even worse, the she-cat ached to sink her teeth into the man's flesh and claim him as her own.

Slut.

It had to be the whole "make-me-into-a-hairy-lioness" thing that had the two of them on edge. What else could the reason be?

Alex lowered his head and kept his mouth shut, and staring at the man before her only made Maya want to snap at him, rip his head clean off. Where was his fucking groveling, damn it?

When no such words were forthcoming, she figured she might as well let him have it. "Alex, you goddamn—"

"Baby, please..."

She snapped her teeth at him, and her beast inside was in agreement. Just because her lioness wanted to mount the handsome man like a bronco, it didn't mean that he'd get off easy. Heh-heh. Get off.

"Don't *baby* me. Where was I? Ahem... Was there a tiny little detail you failed to mention last night, Alex? Like, maybe the fact that last night wasn't just some run-of-the-mill sex fest, but more like your semiannual "get-every-fertile-girl-pregnant" party? Or, let me see, the small fact that your *little* nibble that pierced my skin was a mating mark, and now, because of it, my she-bitch is stuck with your lyin' ass?" Her tone of voice rose higher and higher with each question, until she started to yell. "Oh, I dunno. That, that I'd grow fucking fur, and have the urge to eat my best friend! Huh? What about that? What do you have to say for yourself?"

The man before her narrowed his eyes and had the balls to growl. "I'm sorry."

"Sorry? That's it? Yes, well, that just makes things so much better." She bit out the words and planted her hands on her hips.

"Damn it, Maya. I wanted you from the moment you walked through the doors. The very second your scent hit me I was hooked, and the instant I tasted you, I knew you'd be mine forever."

"You expect me to believe you? How...why?" She blinked back the tears welling up in her eyes, overcome with emotions. So many parts of her warred with one another. Could she trust him? Should she trust him? He hadn't been honest from the start...

But the lioness within...stupid fucking cat craved him like her next breath.

"He's telling the truth, My."

Maya spun and faced the interloper, body instinctively at the ready. She relaxed when she realized it was just Carly.

"But..." Carly quieted her with a glare. Damn her.

"You may not know everything there is to know about furballs, but you, and now your cat, should know that he's telling the truth. Hell, if you weren't inside a makeshift butcher shop, with the remnants of raw meat strewn about, you'd be able to smell it on him."

She quirked a brow. "Really? I'll be able to tell if he's lyin', just by his scent?"

"Yup. And also...if he's been with another woman." Carly nodded.

"Ooh...that's promising."

A low snarl snagged Maya's attention. "I'd *never* cheat on you."

"Carly?"

"It's true." Her friend shook her head. "If he's really your mate, which I believe he is, then no, he won't." Carly turned bright red in the face and gestured at Alex. "His, uh, equipment, would be less than useful."

Maya snorted, the idea of Alex not being able to perform, whatever the reason, seemed rather hilarious to her. The previous night he'd been insatiable, taking her time and again without much rest in between.

"Fine." Maya sighed deep. "I suppose I'll believe him. For now." She took a few steps toward her friend, careful to dodge the bits of meat her kitty hadn't gobbled up. "I'm sorry I tried to eat you, and not in very fun way." Maya opened her arms and hugged her best friend, happy that the cat in her didn't perk up at the idea of having Carly for dinner. "And thanks for not letting me eat Andrew. Or Ian. Or the people in the parking lot. Or…"

Laughing, Carly pulled back a little, but didn't release her hold on Maya. "As if I'd let you end up in furball jail. And not when they won't let you have your *boy toy* behind bars."

Maya pulled her friend close once again, stiffening when she heard growls and snarls from behind. Fast as, well, a lioness, she spun and placed her still nude body between Carly and her…mate? "Alex…" Her voice deepened. "Back off."

Her mate narrowed his eyes. "Quit touching her."

Maya snorted. "What? You think I'm suddenly lesbian because I hugged my friend? Are you on drugs? Seriously?" She huffed, puffed. "I may be tied to you for my suddenly long life, asshole, but you're not going to get all *pissy* whenever I happen to touch someone else."

"No touching. I can't take it. The beast…it can't take it."

A single finger tapped her shoulder. "Uh, My, you should listen to him. He's a little too furry for my taste, but I really don't want to be on the lion's menu. Remember? Mates and stuff? We've talked about this. He's on edge, and you should, you know, humor him for a smidge."

Maya crossed her arms over her chest and glared at him when his attention shifted from her face to her breasts. Men! Ugh. "How long is a smidge? And how much humoring are we talking about? I wanted a one-night stand, Carly. Not a fucking Neanderthal who thinks he owns me. And he has his fucking dick hanging out for heaven's sake!"

The she-cat inside her purred at her last comment. Horny cat.

Maya watched in fascination as fur receded from each of his pores that coated his arms and chest. He then picked up his clothes and slipped them back on, neatly tucking his cock back into his pants and zipping them up. Okay, so maybe he was the tiniest bit pissy. And *maybe* it was because she'd pushed a little too hard. But damn it, she'd had good reason!

"No, I don't own you, Maya..."

"Don't talk to the boobs, buddy." She clicked her fingers to encourage him to raise his gaze. "Up here. Look at my face."

He huffed. "I don't own you, but the cat is...possessive."

She sniffed, realizing she had the same sort of possessive-y feelings, too. But she sure wasn't going to admit that out loud. Nope. Not yet, anyway. *"Fine."*

"And I'm sorry I didn't explain things last night." That was like the third or fourth or fifth apology, she didn't know which, but perhaps he actually was...sorry.

She edged a little closer. Okay, she could deal with the apologies. Apologies were nice when sincere, and her little cat was rubbing against her mind, telling Maya she'd be more than happy to rub all over Alex. "Thanks. I accept your apology."

"And I promise to never whip my dick out...unless you ask for it." His lips twitched and she glared at him.

Maya returned, "And what about the claim-y, bite-y thing?"

"I can't apologize for the act, but I absolutely should've talked to you first."

She nodded. "Good." She tried to be mad, tried to show how upset she still was, but her body wouldn't allow her to—she was drained.

That settled, she invaded his personal space, rested her face against his broad chest.

"Huh? What're you? I mean..." Alex sputtered.

Aw, poor little confused lion. Her human half was still pretty damn angry, but she'd at least forgive him...just a little.

"Come on cat-boy. I figure we've got some talking to do, and I'm starting to get hungry again with all this meat lying around. Speaking of which, Carly..."

Her best friend squeaked and rushed up the stairs, heavy footsteps trailing in her wake. Maya followed, but only made it two steps before a muscular arm wrapped around her waist and tugged her back. "You're not going up there like that." Alex's words were nearly indiscernible, like his lion had wrenched control in that moment.

Maya growled at his firm tone, the she-cat not at all happy with being manhandled, and her annoyance came through, loud and clear, in her voice. "*Well,* seeing as my clothes got shredded during my first shift, when I didn't even know I was a shifter, I didn't have much of a choice this time either, did I?"

Alex released her, spun her around, and replied, "No man but me sees you naked, Maya. No one. I'll cut out the man's eyes rather than let him glimpse a single part of your naked body."

Maya smirked. The lioness reveled in his possessiveness, and she had to admit, the woman did, too. "Fine. But you're buying me new clothes."

"Done."

Huh. Too bad everything else in her life couldn't be fixed this easily.

* * *

Shit, fuck, damn, and growl.

Okay, at least, Alex had managed to get Maya out of the buck's house without exposing any more of her lush body than he had to, thanks to Carly and her enormous wardrobe. And hey, they'd even snagged some new clothes for Maya at the mall.

At least, the shopping was done, and his relatively sweet mate was well-clothed. And dare he say, semi-happy. Semi, because he'd brought her back to Genesis, and partially against her will.

"I'm not going in there." Maya balked at the door and dug her heels in.

Alex clenched his teeth and fisted his hands. "Please, my sweet. The pride would like to meet you, and besides, being around them will calm your lioness."

She sighed deep. For the umpteenth time. Damn it, she'd been doing that a lot with him, and his cat was pissed that the man couldn't do a freaking thing right.

"Fine, I'll go. You know, all you have to do is explain things to me. Preferably before you want me to do something."

With a nod he pulled open the front door and the comforting scent of his pride surrounded them, soothed his inner cat.

Until Jenner ran to meet them that was, tripping over his lovesick feet with every step he took toward Maya. "Prime! Oh, you found her!"

Good god, man. Alex hoped he wouldn't have to deal with all the males tripping over themselves to get close to Maya. Then, he'd have to kill them. Not really, but he hoped he didn't have to make a choice.

The rest of the pride trailed in Jenner's wake in a swarm, each of them anxious to meet their new prima. They were all cleaned up and ready for her arrival, thank goodness. Though she hadn't yet claimed him, he'd already bitten her, and that was more than enough to ensure the pride's initial acceptance of her.

In a flash they were surrounded by their lions and lionesses, males and females alike nuzzling her shoulder and inhaling her scent. Alex's beast approved. The pride had to learn their prima's scent and remember it always, let her essence be entwined with their cats'.

Alex stood back and watched as his pride accepted her, welcoming her with open arms. Every so often Maya's head would raise, turn to look over the crowd to search him out, and then she'd settle, returning her attention to those around her.

Damn, something writhed in his chest, tightened and scratched at the display before him. Twenty, thirty years ago and he woulda laughed if anyone had told him he'd be taking a mate, but now, there was nothing funny about the woman who was being rejoiced by his pride. With her flowing blonde hair and luscious curves, he'd mated to the Venus incarnate.

And he couldn't wait to bed her again, to have her teeth against his shoulder so that she could claim him. Okay, he'd even beg if it were necessary. Anything to have the tempting goddess reciprocate his feelings, to help calm the damned lion that resided within.

As he watched Gina eased away from the group fawning over Maya and came toward him. Her head bowed the lion was pleased to find that the woman showed some contrition. He'd confined her to her home, but a pride meeting superseded all other orders.

"Prime." The woman tilted her head to the side to expose her neck, making herself vulnerable to him.

"Gina." He wouldn't allow her to know his feelings. True, she'd fucked up royally, and all for spite, but still, he'd gotten his mate because she'd gone against him.

Gina raised her head, her gaze fixated on his chest. "I-I'm sorry for my behavior. I understand that there will be consequences for my actions. All I can do is beg, for you and the pride, to forgive me."

Alex grunted. The cat within scented the truthfulness of her words, but the man couldn't help but remember how he'd found his mate in the basement that'd been practically painted with raw meat, with Maya ready to eat her friend for dinner.

"The entire pride will hear your apology this evening. Though, I am hesitant to punish you any further, since your actions resulted in me meeting my mate."

Gina raised her gaze in a split-second, and jumped into his arms the next, enveloping him in a tight hug as she nuzzled his neck. Alex accepted the woman's action for what it was—a reaffirmation of their pride bond—and also Gina's way of assuring herself that all was forgiven.

Maya, unfortunately, did not.

Between one blink and the next the woman was ripped from his body and thrown against the floor. Maya used her newly acquired reflexes, crouching over the fallen woman before Alex had the chance to speak a single word. She caught Gina by the throat and Alex watched, thoroughly rapt, as his sweet mate half shifted. Her face elongated, a snout partially formed, her fingers changed into razor-sharp claws.

The prima, his better half, snarled one word and one word only, "*Mine.*"

Thank fucking god. About time.

With careful steps Alex approached his crouching mate, unwilling to startle his little lioness. He recognized Maya's behavior for what it was, too—that it was a showing of possession and dominance for all of her pride to see.

It was probably wrong that this made him hard, right?

Now next to Maya he eased down and looked at the two women. His mate was nothing short of beautiful in her half shift, as she was in any other form she chose, looking fierce and deadly and simply stunning.

Damn, this really got him hot.

A glance at Gina revealed that the woman was deathly pale, eyes wide and mouth hanging open, gasping for air. Tiny rivulets of blood slid down the woman's neck from where his mate had punctured her skin.

"Maya, love. It's not nice to kill one of your own on the first day." She snarled at him, gaze never leaving her target. He cleared his throat. "Mate, why don't we go upstairs and you can claim me. Show the rest of the females that I belong to you. You'd like that, right?" 'Cause he sure as hell would.

She narrowed her eyes and tilted her head toward him as if weighing his words. He held his breath, waited for her to respond. The cat in her had been riding her hard, no doubt for the last ten hours or so, and he wasn't sure which way she'd go. Punish, or show mercy.

Then, Maya released her grip on Gina's throat and pounced on him, clinging to him like a damned spider monkey, shredding his shirt just before a fierce pain gripped his shoulder, yanking a harrowing cry from deep within his chest. Fuck, fire enveloped him, but he didn't dare move. Shit, shit, shit.

His woman had bitten him, marking him, the thumping of his heart pushing the ache into his limbs. And he just waited, waited for her to regain control, to let her finish what she started. A few beats of his heart passed, and then a few more, before Maya eased her hold, and finally, her thick, sharp fangs slid free of his flesh. His whole body shuddered in response, the pain lessening with each breath as she lapped at his wound.

Well. At least, Alex finally got what he wanted. And now, he and his lion, belonged to her, till death do them part.

Chapter Six

Hah! Alex belonged to her now! Take that bitches!

Wait. Were she-cats considered bitches?

The lioness could tell that the skinny bitch wanted her mate, but she couldn't get her claws into Maya's man. Oh, nonono. Not after all that she'd endured since bedding Alex.

Maya's lioness felt the urge to flick dirt over the frightened woman, and bury her the same way she'd bury bodily waste. But she wouldn't. Regardless of the woman's actions toward her man, Maya was now part of the pride. And she'd do her best to act like the prima she was. Yeah, sure, blah, blah, blah...and all that queenly stuff she'd no doubt have to do now. Though, one more snuggle and rub against Alex by that woman, and all bets would've been off. She'd go crouching lion, hidden *biatch* on the lioness' ass. Grrr, roar, huff, and puff.

Maya, at the urging of her beast, lapped some more at the damage she'd done, slowed the bleeding on her mate's shoulder. She growled against his skin, "Mine."

"Yeah, baby. I am. As you are mine."

She purred, relaxed, body getting hot with his affirmation. God, the taste of him on her tongue, his heat, it all coalesced, growing within, until she *needed* him. Just had to have him. Fuck, it felt as if she had a shit-ton of problems weighing heavy on her shoulders, but the cat rubbing from beneath her skin didn't seem to give a damn. And the more her cat purred and pleaded, the more Maya found that her human side was nearly onboard with taking Alex to bed.

Maya nuzzled his neck, scented him, inhaled the unique smells of her mate. She licked him again, savoring the citrus and cinnamon flavor that burst across her taste buds. She repeated, "Mm...*mine.*"

Her pussy ached and grew damper by the second. Oh, yeah, she was totally onboard now...more than ready for some one-on-one time with her man. At this very moment in time it didn't matter that they were practically strangers. So maybe Maya was quick to forgive, and even quicker to love, but truth be told, she hadn't an ounce of anger left in her for the man she clung to—she was his prima and he was her prime.

Alex stroked her back. "I'm yours. Now, why don't we quit putting on a show for the pride and take this upstairs."

Ooh, that was the best idea he'd had all day. He must've read her mind.

Without a word she rolled to her feet and tugged him along, leading him toward the stairs, a hoarse laugh trailing behind them. Surprisingly, she easily recognized the source. *Grayson.* And there was even more laughing, presumably because his second wasn't used to seeing the prime being led by a woman.

Halfway up the steps the lioness was over the damned laughing hyena... She whirled and bared her teeth at the crowd, a loud hiss escaping her lips. "Enough!"

Silence...

"Damn, baby, you just made my dick hard."

Oh. *Oh.* She leaned back against him, rubbed her ass over his bulging erection.

"Come on, sweetheart, I have a feeling that Grayson's done laughing."

With a nod she resumed her climb, Alex trailing in her wake. She shoved the door open, jerked him inside, and then shut it behind them with a resounding slam, blanketing the two of them in darkness. The scent of their sex from the previous night still hung in the air, tugged and pulled at her inner cat, until every thought in Maya's head revolved around either taking, or getting taken by, her mate.

Flicking on the light she worked to adjust her dilated pupils. When focused, her gaze took in the man who stood before her, just as gorgeous as the night before, wearing a skin-tight shirt and formfitting jeans, cloth outlining his muscles, causing saliva to gather in her mouth. *I will not drool.*

His amber eyes darkened as the seconds ticked by. She licked her lips, the she-cat inside remembering the taste of his blood. She consciously let her hands shift, nails lengthening and forming into deadly claws. But she didn't have death on her mind. No, she zeroed in on his skin.

Maya took a step forward and he retreated. She took another, and once again, Alex stepped back. She stalked him, a delicate dance between new mates...

"Alex..." The lioness needed him to stop. Not wanted, but *needed.*

"Come along, mate." He smirked at her, making a "come here" motion with his fingers.

Oh, how she'd love to have those skillful digits inside her again. Damn, the idea of being filled by him and rubbing her G-spot, sent a shiver of arousal shooting down her spine.

She playfully growled as he continued to move away from her, as more and more space separated them. The cat was getting tired of waiting, and wasn't against using her newly acquired speed to her advantage. So, Maya shot forward and threw her weight into the pounce, forcing Alex to the ground with a heavy thud. Her body sprawled atop his—with her knees on either side of his hips—she now had her man exactly where she wanted him.

A motorboat-like purr filled her chest. "Maya…"

She nuzzled his neck, his scent filling her lungs, stoking her need. She ached to have her mate filling and pleasuring her, while they claimed each other once again. Yes, the bites were exchanged, but their mating ritual hadn't exactly gone down the normal route. At least, that was what her lioness told her. And that it was high time they made it right.

She lapped at his neck, gathered his sweet-sweat taste on her tongue, flicked over the now-healing bite of his shoulder. A shudder wracked Alex's body and Maya realized the wound must be his hotspot. *Interesting*.

Placing her hands on his chest she levered herself up until she sat up on his groin, the hard line of his cock nudging her from beneath. Oh, yes. With one hand she pulled at the center of his shirt, slicing down the front of it with a single claw, baring her mate's upper torso to her gaze. Inch-by-inch the hard planes of his chest were revealed to her, and she found herself desperate for another taste. She wanted to bite and nibble every part of him, mark him from head-to-toe to warn others away from her mate.

"Maya," he growled as he gripped her hips, pushing down as he ground his cloth-covered cock against her. "I'm trying to be patient, baby. But I'm hanging on by a thread. Please...please...can you just give me a little something?"

Oh, damn, she could certainly get used to his begging.

Most definitely.

With a wicked smile she rose to her feet, stared down at her man's fierce gaze. With quick, efficient movements, she whipped her shirt off, and then used her claws to shred her new skirt and panties from her body. And though he seemed desperate to have her, Maya too, was just as needy as Alex.

She wasn't sure where this newfound bravado was coming from, but she wasn't going to second-guess herself now. And though she had curves upon luscious curves, Alex looked at her like she was a goddess he wanted to worship at the altar.

Maya tugged control from her cat, forced her hands to resume their human shape, then slid a single finger between her breasts, cupped the plump globe, kneaded the flesh and plucked and pinched her hardened nipple. The hint of a sting inched her arousal higher, causing her pussy to clench, tighten and release more of her musky scent into the air.

Alex licked his lips, staring at her like he was staring at his first plate of food after being rescued from a deserted island.

"Like what you see, huh, lion-o?"

He nodded slowly, his gaze transfixed on her bare breasts.

Maya stepped back some, feet still straddling him, until she could crouch over and reach the waist of his pants. She traced the line of his hard dick, the long shaft that was held captive within his jeans. Poor baby. She palmed his cock through his jeans, delighting as it throbbed and twitched in her hand.

"You ready for me, Alex?"

He growled, but didn't utter a word.

She wasn't sure she could keep the lioness back any longer. The damned bitch wanted to wrench control away from her, and claim the lion properly.

All in good time.

With a flick of her fingers she popped the button on his jeans, and then tugged the zipper down, ever-so-slowly. More and more of his flesh was exposed to her, causing her mouth to water, just aching for a taste of his flesh.

She wanted him filling and stretching her needy pussy more than anything. Damn, it'd only been hours, but she desired to have him again. And again. And again.

Alex snarled from below and she stroked his rippling abdomen, petting and soothing him. "Soon, mate. Soon."

He settled, but kept his narrowed eyes trained on her. She admired the level of control he exhibited. Her she-cat recognized Alex's dominance, but also appreciated his passive behavior.

Hooking her fingers beneath the waist of his pants she stood and eased them down his legs, stopping only long enough to rid him of his shoes, before working to get him completely nude.

She then crawled over his bare body, rubbed and nuzzled her way along his legs, stopping when her face met his groin. His dick was hard for her, standing tall with a tiny droplet of pre-cum shining at the tip. Part of her, the horny cat slut side, wanted to lap at his cream. But the other part wanted him inside her pussy first.

Maya continued her travels along his body until her hips hovered over his, the tip of his dick teasing along her soaking slit, petting her with his spongy head, making her shudder on contact.

"Oh, Alex..." She really did purr—a vocal representation of absolute contentment.

"Maya, it better be soon...or you're going to get fucked hard, whether you like it or not." A thrill raced through her then, filling every inch and then some. But even her lioness recognized the "threat" in his aggressive words.

She reached beneath her, grasped his heated shaft and positioned his swollen crown at the entrance to her heat. With infinite care she lowered herself, let him fill and stretch her, touch her electrified nerves, inch-by-pleasurable-inch.

Alex slid his palms along her thighs, not rushing her, just touching and stroking her skin, making her hotter and hotter. Then, lower and lower she fell, as more and more of him spread her pussy wide, until her hips rested against his, her cunt throbbing and pulsing around his satisfying invasion.

Breathing heavy she leaned forward, changed the angle of penetration and caressed his chest with the palms of her hands, sifted her fingers through the downy fur that'd formed during her playful torture. Oh, her fierce lion was already nearing the edge.

Alex gripped her hips, fingers digging into her plump flesh, the pinpricks of pain telling her that his digits had become claws. Her she-cat purred and rolled onto her back from within, thrilled that she'd pushed her mate this far.

Deciding to give her lover some relief she raised her hips, heat dragging along his shaft, yanking a groan from inside his chest. Vibrations traveled along his cock, transferring to her, through her, intensifying her need to heights she'd never reached before.

"Fuck, Maya," he hissed. The pain at her hips increased, and at the same time, the burning ache in her pussy caused her to clamp down hard on his dick. "Fuck me, sweet lioness."

She giggled, smiling down at him. "That's what I'm doing."

Rising, her pussy lips reached the tip, then she quickly reversed course, taking him back into her hole again, nice and slow, feeling his length pushing on her walls as she slid all the way down. Then she moved back up and down again, repeating the rising and falling motion of her hips, her body loving each of his pleasure-filled invasions, all as her pussy released more of her juices, coating them both in her feminine glaze. She flexed her re-formed claws and pierced his skin, the scent of their blood misting the air.

God, the hint of his essence called to her cat, causing her canines to elongate, piercing her gums as they grew. And Maya increased the pace of her fucking, shuddering with every meeting of their hips, his pelvis hitting her clit just right, ratcheting her desire to feverish heights. Her pussy convulsed, twitched as it milked him, the tremors of her impending climax dancing wildly through her, faster and higher with each passing second.

Panting, she fucked quicker still, the sounds of their flesh meeting filling the room, mingling with their heavy pants. Alex used his grip to increase the force of her movements, slamming her down against him, his hips rising to meet her descending thrusts.

One of her hands abandoned his chest, moving to her breast to massage it, tugging on her nipple just hard enough to feel a pinch. Her pussy responded immediately, and her clit throbbed right along with the thunderous beating of her heart. She moaned, her gaze intent on Alex's, imagining that the color of her eyes mirrored his fiery gold, their arousal a palpable presence in the room.

At some point Alex had stolen the control away from her, as he now held her hips steady, furiously pumping his cock into her from below, pounding her aching pussy while giving her the pleasure she so desperately craved.

"Yes, yes, yes..." She needed him, desired him like no other before, and her she-cat was readily in agreement.

The man loving her from below was hers. *Hers*. No other lioness would ever dare steal him away. If they cared for their lives...

"Come for me, kitten. Come on my cock and I'll claim you again."

She growled, the idea sending her excitement soaring, her orgasm running toward her, swift, like a lioness chasing her prey. She bared her teeth at Alex, answering him with the primal sound of her beast, annoyed by his order, regardless of the fact that she really did want to come. More than anything.

"Quit your bitching, she-cat, and come for me." He growled and snarled at her, and the lioness inside accepted his dominance.

Maya panted and purred as her climax was nearly within reach, her lioness prowling inside, itching to be free. Seconds passed as her approaching orgasm abruptly brought her to the precipice, trying its damnedest to hurl her over the edge.

"Gonna come in your pussy as soon as you come for me, kitten. Do it... Claim me again my lovely she-cat. My beautiful lioness."

With a fierce, explosive snarl and roar her pussy convulsed, until one spasm melted into the next, over and over again, faster and faster as she tiptoed on the edge. Her climax was so close. Right there, and yet...

Then, Alex shifted his hold, brought a finger to her clit and strummed the sensitive nub, the tip of his claw gently scraping against the bundle of nerves. And that was all it took, all she needed to find her release.

Her orgasm overtook her, slammed into her like a thousand explosions, a wild eruption that stole what was left of her control. So Maya let go, gave in, doing the only thing that would surely make her beast happy. She leaned forward, snarl on her lips, and she struck like lightening, sinking her teeth into her mate's flesh in a flash, biting into his pec until his blood filled her mouth.

An answering shot of pain hit her like a sledgehammer, when Alex's teeth sank deep into her shoulder, the bit of hurt intensifying her bliss tenfold. Wave after wave of rapture coalesced, exploding within the confines of her skin, her she-cat roaring as ecstasy filled her from head-to-toe. The bitch reveled in their renewed, proper claiming.

Before her orgasm fully receded the delightful sensations of her climax stole her breath away once more. She was a ball of feeling and need, pleasure like lava coursing through her fiery veins.

Distantly, she heard Alex give in to his own release, felt his dick pulse and throb within her quivering pussy, his hot cum coating her inner walls. The she-cat, her lioness, relished the idea of being filled with his cubs.

Alex stroked her back, gentling her as the tremors eased, and when she finally returned from the pleasure-filled haze, she realized her teeth were still firmly embedded in his chest.

With infinite care she slid her canines free and lapped at the broken skin, wincing when she saw the damage she'd caused. "Sorry." Another lick, a soft kiss, and she pushed herself up so she could better inspect the injury. "Really, really sorry."

Alex, her mate, just smiled. Smug bastard. "I'm not. It'll tell all those other females that I'm taken."

She snorted and draped over him, snuggled as close as she could, savoring the fact that he was still inside her, still filling her, even as his cock softened. She raised her head, propped her chin on his chest. "So, what now?"

He wrapped his arms around her waist, held her even closer if that were possible. "Now... now you become my love slave, worship me forever, and give me lots of little Maya cubs to spoil."

"Pft." She blew a raspberry. "Keep dreaming, lion-o. How about, you become *my* love slave, worship *me* forever, and have all the little furballs I give ya?"

"A little difficult without the right equipment, no?"

"What-*evah,*" she grumbled. "Fine. Here's my last offer. Yes to everlasting love, someday...just not quite yet, but hey, I'm your mate, right? We have all the time in the world, so there's no rush. *No* to the slave or the worshipping, but the furballs are negotiable."

He leaned forward and lightly brushed his lips across hers. "I'm lucky to have you, Maya. And Prima?

"Hm?"

"You are absolutely perfect, just the way you are."

"Heh. You ain't lyin'."

The End

YOU'RE LION

You're Lion

God save Maya from every overprotective, pigheaded, butt sniffing, meddling men—even if they were lions.

Argh.

What could be the source of her frustration? Perhaps it had something to do with the five—count 'em, *five*—werelions guarding her, while she waited her turn at the gyno's office. To make things that much more unbearable, each one of 'em looked ready to pounce on and destroy anyone or anything that came within a few feet of her. Great. Just the sorta thing that these pregnant woman needed in their already difficult lives. Surely, she thought.

The door on the other side of the room opened and a familiar woman poked her head out. Maya immediately recognized her as one of the nurses, and breathed a huge thank-fucking-god sigh of relief when she heard her name called.

"Maya Josephs?"

Her quintet of "guard dogs" responded in unison. "It's O'Connell."

Maya rolled her eyes, unable—or maybe unwilling—to stop the growl that roared from her chest. She gave her inner furball lioness bitch a mental high five for that sound of hostility. She'd be damned if she took her mate's name just yet. Both sides of her—human and she-cat alike—were pretty pissed about the lack of something sparkly on the ring finger of her left hand. It'd been months since their mating—which he'd done on the sly by the way, *thankyouverymuch,* and Maya was still without the customary ring she could flash to all of her non-furry friends. The other shifters had congratulated her on their mating, but her human friends were left to wonder when she and Alex would be getting hitched.

Maya was still having the whole "last name" argument with the entire effing pride it seemed. And, as far as she was concerned, until she and Alex said their "I dos," she was gonna cling to Josephs like she was a starving Spider Monkey that held the last banana in the freakin' jungle.

"Um, Miss Josephs?" The nurse raised her brows and Maya hopped to her feet, before the "Fearsome Fivesome," as she jokingly named them, could interject (again), and practically ran toward the door.

Of course, the idjits just couldn't let her go get her "hoo-ha" examined alone. Nope, they all charged after her, no doubt scaring the poor nurse silly, since the woman suddenly bolted from the doorway the moment Maya reached for the knob. Before stepping into the gyno office's inner domain, she turned and faced her unneeded—and unwanted— werelion guards (because, really? Who in the hell was going to come after little ol' her, especially at the doctor's office?) and glared at them en masse. "No. Bad kitties. Sit. *Stay.*"

"But—" started Wyatt.

"Prima..." Deuce chimed in.

"The Prime said—" Harding added.

"Alex gave us strict orders," Neal interrupted.

Then, a gruff voice rose above the rest. "Leave her be."

The last three words came from her favorite "babysitter," Brute, (whose real name was Brutus, but nobody called him that, for fear of being beaten to a bloody pulp by his deadly hands), and she jumped at his uttered orders as if they were a freaking lifeline.

"Super! I'll see y'all in a bit!"

With a forced smile and a quick wave, she chased after the nurse, leaving five grumbling werelions in the crowded waiting area. She felt bad for the pregnant women who'd be surrounded by all of that testosterone. Well, mostly sorry, at any rate. Because, only two people in the world were allowed to see her vagina, damn it. The man who fucked it stupid (thank god for that), and the man who made sure it stayed healthy. The quintet would just have to wait outside.

After a quick weigh-in (she opted not to look) and a check of her blood pressure (you go healthy chubby chick!), the nurse led her to the bathroom to pee in a cup. Now that she was sexually active, she had to endure the whole pregnancy-check-thingie before they'd give her another quarterly birth control shot. Whatever. She'd pee until the cows came home if it meant that she and Alex could continue to forgo the use of condoms.

Whee!

Her business finished, Maya headed over to the exam room and frowned at the folded paper outfit resting on the table. Ugh. She rather hated getting nekkid here, and being wrapped up in a thin, napkin-like sheet didn't make her feel any better.

No way to avoid it, though.

After making sure the door was nice and secure, she stripped and donned the provided flimsy gown, then plopped her jiggly ass on the exam table and waited. And waited some more. Man, she really hoped one of the doctor's patients wasn't in labor. 'Cause gynos were notoriously known for being called away to do the whole push-push-push-catch-thing.

After what felt like forever, a soft knock sounded, and the man of the hour, Doc Molloy, poked his head in. "Ready for me?"

Pre-Alex, Maya had had a love-hate relationship with her gynecologist. On one hand, Dr. Molloy was uber hawt. But on the other, she'd had to strip buck naked and let him poke at her vag…and not in a very fun way, mind you. Shit, he'd never even bought her dinner first.

Presently, her lioness hated the human male, and wanted to scratch his face off for even thinking of touching her. Apparently, that was how mated she-cats responded to the men that weren't their mates.

Huh.

"Yup. Ready as I'll ever be." She smiled, simply because it was that, or hiss and growl at him, something that her lioness was itching to do.

Upset kitty was clawing at her insides, growling, hissing, and spitting, protesting the presence of the male…especially because of the reason why the stranger was there. The doc stepped fully into the room and closed them inside the small space, his focus fixed on her chart as he settled onto a nearby stool. Which was kinda weird. She was visiting for a quick shot of hormones to prevent pregnancy. And typically, that involved a quick boob check, a needle in the ass, and then the doc taking a seat to jot some notes down. Wham, bam, bill the insurance please, ma'am.

He *did not* sit down to chat first.

Nevah.

"So... I'm going to go out on a limb and say that there must be a new man in your life, and that you're sexually active now. According to my notes, the last time you were here, it says that you had just gotten out of a relationship." He then proceeded to do the whole "raise a single brow" thing.

Well, she could pull that trick, too. Maya mimicked his move, working at looking all confident and whatnot, regardless of the embarrassing state of her current wardrobe. Being confident was something Alex was teaching her. "What makes you say that?"

Dr. Molloy smirked and raised his eyebrow again. It was like he'd had plenty of lessons on how to grin and do the eyebrow-thingie at the same time. "Well... The fact that you're pregnant, Maya, is what."

What the...? Well... Shit, fuck, damn, and growl.

* * *

An hour later, and with plenty of hyperventilating to boot, Maya sneakily slipped out of the doc's back entrance and into the parking lot where—praisejesushallelujahamen—a yellow cab was fortuitously waiting.

Because, really... She totally was not ready to face the quintet, or their prying questions. Nor did she want to get hauled back home to Alex. Because there was a pretty good chance she would've broken down and cried, then slugged the shit out of him for knocking her up. How in the fuckity-fuck? Besides, telling her babies that she'd given her father a black eye upon learning of her pregnancy, would so not be a happy story for her future little ones to hear.

The hell? She'd been boinking Alex sans condoms because 1) shifters didn't carry diseases, and 2) she was on the damn birth control shot.

No one, not even Alex, had told her that furballs had super sperm that could muck with her system and get her preggers.

Grrr…

Dr. Molloy had had way too much fun teasing her about the facts of life while he peeked at her vag. In her full-on state of disbelief, she'd immediately demanded a sonogram, because the shot had suppressed her monthly visitor since she'd begun the damn birth control cycle.

Twelve friggin' weeks… She was that far along, which put her conception date right at the time of their mating.

Fucking Alex. And stupid fucking super sperm, too. Why was she so upset? Was it shock? Disbelief? Hormones? Shouldn't she be the least bit happy?

Well, at least the she-cat was jumping up and down, screaming "Woo-hoo babies!" over and over again, rolling around on her back in pure joy, exposing her soon-to-be growing belly and purring to high heaven. Traitorous furry biatch.

Acting on hormonal instinct, Maya directed the cabbie to an address she knew well. Her best friend Carly would calm her down, she thought. At least, enough so that when she finally did see Alex, Maya would be less apt to go after his junk, to prevent him from doing this to her without her consent, or knowledge, ever again. She was certain he must've known about his super sperm.

Speaking of the little tadpoles...

They couldn't just get her pregnant. Nooo, that would've been too easy. Instead, she'd learned that he'd knocked her up with twins.

A freakin' litter.

Gah!

Minutes that felt like hours taking their merry-ass time, finally passed. Thankfully, the cabbie pulled up to the front of Carly's house. Not so long ago, three months to be more concise, her BFF had helped her through her first shift and had kept her safe, almost getting eaten alive by a turning Maya in the process—and not in a very good way mind you, but in a very, very bad way for all her trouble.

Back then, Maya's she-cat had felt that the rabbit shifter should've been on the lioness' menu. But now, while Maya still couldn't control her actual shift for shit (mostly), she could at least keep the beast from wanting to chow down (sadly for Carly, in a totally non-lesbian way) on her furry friend.

Maya tossed a handful of bills (because, really, who could count when they've just been shocked with the news that they were pregnant with a litter) at the driver, and then raced to her friend's front door as fast as her high-heeled feet would carry her.

Momentum building and rather unsure if she could stop, now that'd she'd worked up a full head of steam, Maya was hella happy when the door swung open, with a stunned-looking Carly meeting her before she managed to plow into the steel entrance. "M?"

"Glad you're home," Maya quickly returned. She skidded to a stop once inside the entryway, slick bottoms of her shoes sliding over the polished hardwood floors. She was reminded that she needed to get the sole-grippy-thingamajigs. "I'm pregnant, Carly. How could *you* not know that I was pregnant? How in the hell did everyone's super sniffers not pick up on that, huh? I mean, pregnant, Carly. Carrying. Gestating. Breeding. Dear god, please help me." She sucked in a much needed breath to try to calm her frazzled nerves. "And to think... I'm preggers with a litter!"

And then, her very best friend in the whole wide world, ever since they were six years old, when they'd pinky sworn to be *bestest* friends forevah, later becoming blood sisters with the whole owie-owie-exchange-of-blood-thing, laughed her furry little rabbit ass off. And then... Carly laughed some more. Maya could've sworn the lightest scent of urine drifted toward her.

Oh, my god. The bitch fucking peed herself.

Heffer. Rabbit heffer...but still a heffer, goddamnit.

"I'd..." Carly snorted, "...I'd offer you some wine to calm down, but pregnant women aren't supposed to drink." Then, Ms. Rabbit Heffer chuckled some more.

Wow, just wow. Maya was speechless. She wondered which was worse—her friend making light of her serious situation, or the fact that Carly wet her pants.

Ignoring her soon-to-be *ex-best friend,* she stormed past Carly and ventured deeper into the house and went straight into the kitchen—specifically, to her friend's freezer, where she knew her friend had some goodies.

Between the front door and the ice cream haven that was her rabbit friend's ice box, tingling and pinching pain encompassed her hands, the nails shifting from perfectly manicured to razor-sharp claws.

Apparently, her lioness was just as excited as Maya was about Chunky Monkey ice cream.

In the blink of an eye—okay, maybe more than a blink—she wrapped her palm around the freezer's handle and ripped the door clean off. Like, completely. One second the freezer had been closed, and the next, it was minus a door. Huh. Her inner cat must be more eager for ice cream than she'd thought.

"Maya!"

She ignored Carly. Maya had a quart of Ben & Jerry's in her sights, and nothing was going to deter her now. She snatched the container and spun to face her friend, snarl on her lips. "*Mine. Grrr...*"

Carly's eyebrows rose, almost retreating into her hairline. "Uh, yeah, okay. Totally cool. I so didn't want a door on my freezer anyway. Look, it's all 'shabby chic' now."

She watched the smaller woman inch around the kitchen and dig into a drawer, then tossed a spoon toward Maya's direction. She snatched it out of the air, then ripped the top off of the pint of heaven and dug right in. The first burst of banana ice cream, mixed with fudge chunks and walnuts exploding in her mouth, was enough to calm the raging beast.

Apparently, the she-cat, while quite pleased of the doctor's news at first, was now hopping on the OMG-I-can't-believe-he-got-me-pregnant-bandwagon. Maya wondered if feeding her cat delicious ice cream had anything to do with it. Took the easily swayed bitch long enough, she thought.

Frozen bit of relief firmly in her hands, she slumped into a nearby chair with legs sprawled, and kicked off her shoes. Like, literally. *Wha-pow!* She threw them off so hard they crashed into the wall, leaving noticeable dents in their wake.

"By the way," Maya began, getting comfortable, then, "don't answer your phone if it happens to ring, please. I don't want to talk to Alex...or any of his lions right now."

"O...kay..."

"I'm serious, Carly."

"Fine. But you're totally paying to get that fixed. You know that, right? Oh, and let's not forget about my freezer door, you rageaholic."

Half-listening, she waved her spoon at Carly. "Yeah, yeah. Alex, if I let him live, will have someone come over and patch that shit right up for you. But my visit is about making *me* feel all better, so let's *hop* to it." Maya snorted. She could be so funny sometimes. She made a bunny joke. Heh.

"Bitch," Carly fired back.

"Actually, pregnant cats are called *queens*. So, Queen Bitch would be more appropriate, I think." She tilted her head to the side and pondered. "Yeah. I think I kinda dig that."

Carly rolled her eyes. "Whatever. So, we're pregnant, huh?"

"By *we*, you mean *me*, right?" She scooped out another hunk of ice cream and downed it, then pointed the empty spoon at her friend. "'Cause last I knew, you were on a 'dick' boycott. Right?"

Carly stuck out her tongue, then blew raspberries at her like a freakin' child. "Yes. *Anyway*... *You're* pregnant, freaked about it, and now you're here, and surprisingly, without the company of the quintet." The smaller woman grabbed a spoon for herself before inching close enough to steal a scoop of the gooey goodness that Maya was selfishly hoarding. "Speaking of which, I'm thinking about ending the 'weenie' boycott, and I'm totally down with taking one of the fab five off of your hands. I'm thinking Wyatt...or maybe Deuce. Which do you think is better in bed?"

A deep snort, followed quickly by a male grunt interrupted their fun, their OMG-I'm-pregnant-fest, and without looking, Maya immediately knew who that sound belonged to. One of the unshakeable quintet had found her at last. But where were the others?

"I'd say neither, Ms. *Lucky*." Neal poked his head around the corner. "I'm the man to rock your world." The werelion's eyes were a deeper blue than Maya had ever seen. Soon, the unmistakable scent of arousal and desire filled the small space.

Wow. So, *she* could smell something as delicate as arousal, but no one could smell her freakin' pregnancy? What. The. Fuck. Wait, did that make any sense? Besides, Maya hadn't been able to tell a damn thing, either. And she was the one who was pregnant for chrissakes.

Ugh. Grrr. Shit. Fuck everyone, including her.

She pointed at the slick-talking cowboy intruder. "Hey... No, Neal. Bad kitty. That was not a very good rabbit's foot joke. *And*... No cat of mine is allowed to chase my BFF's fluffy tail...unless they've got mating and little kitties on their mind."

Carly glared at her. "You take all the fun out of being your friend, you know that?" She snatched the Chunky Monkey from Maya's hands. "Cock blockers don't deserve to eat my ice cream. None for you!"

Maya tilted her head and pondered. "You mad? I mean, because of the boycott, wouldn't I be a pussy blocker?"

Carly fired back, "That makes absolutely no sense, Maya. Besides, I told you I was thinking about ending it, didn't I?"

* * *

Ever since he'd bonded with Maya, Alex found himself constantly fighting the urge to beat his lions to a pulp, for their inability to keep track of his mate—with painfully surprising frequency.

When he was young, his father had cautioned him about how possessive he'd become toward his future mate, and that he'd find it difficult to let her out of his sight. And he couldn't forget... He'd hate any man who even dared to look at his female.

At the time, young Alex had chuckled, and had professed to his dad that he wouldn't be anything like that. That no woman would wrap the great Alex O'Connell around their finger. Looking back now, it was hard for him to admit how naïve he'd been.

God, he'd been wrong. Insanely wrong.

And it didn't help that he cared for Maya as much as he did. She meant the world to him...and then some.

He pinched the bridge of his nose and closed his eyes, taking deep, relaxing breaths to keep both his lion and human side calm. "Tell me again, Brute, how the five of you managed to lose one female."

"Well, the thing is..." the biggest of the quintet drawled, and it miffed Alex that the lion wasn't shaking with fear. But, his inner cat reminded him that he'd personally selected men who wouldn't cower in the face of danger, men who'd without question put his mate's life before theirs. So yeah, he supposed the lion shouldn't be afraid of him, just respectful. Damn the beast. "Look, Prime, I've got sisters, and I know what happens at one of those *girly parts* appointments. I didn't think you'd want five unmated men staring at your near-naked mate."

The lion had a point. Damn the beast for the second time.

"She escaped through the back, Prime. We tried to reach her, but she turned off—"

"I don't want to hear it, Brute." With a sigh, Alex turned away from the group. He'd handpicked Maya's quintet of guards, wanting to keep her safe from pretty much everything, but he also hadn't exactly counted on his lioness going against his orders, either. She was supposed to take the men with her, wherever she went—that was the deal.

She'd objected to losing her little box of death that was her car, but he'd stood firm, and she finally agreed to let him replace it with a big, safe SUV. She'd demanded one in pink with spinning rims and he'd happily obliged, so long as she didn't put up a fuss about the quintet driving her around. Even to her gynecologist's office.

He checked his watch and winced. Their guests were due to arrive any second now and, since Maya was to be the focus of the Gathering, her absence was certainly not a good thing. Not at all. Alex only hoped his wayward mate would show up before...

Brute interrupted his train of thought. "Besides, Alpha, Neal's with her now. I made the executive decision to split us up, once we caught up with the prima at Carly's. I sent him inside by himself, given how he can smooth-talk just about anyone when he puts his mind to it. Besides, I figured she had a good reason to ditch us the way she did. Anyway, he should be on his way back with her any minute now. I'm sorry, Alex. I just thought that—"

"Never mind, Brute. We'll discuss this later."

Alex sighed deep, overcome with a sense of relief. Her cell was going straight to voicemail, and he was well past alarmed, rapidly on his way to being beside himself. And though he was expecting important guests, he had been seconds away from taking matters into his own hands...even if it had meant getting on Maya's shit list for being overly protective. If only she knew just how far and long he'd searched for his true mate...

Jenner raced around the corner and stumbled toward Alex, limbs flailing like an eager cub. Okay, the boy was just over twenty, and was man enough to have hit on his mate once upon a time, but he was still just a cub in Alex's eyes. He had a bit of growing up and filling out to do, before Alex could even think about seeing the kid as anything else.

"Prime," the lion gasped, "the tiger delegate is here, and members of the Council have just pulled into the driveway."

Shit, fuck, damn, and growl.

I swear to god, I'm going to get my mate microchipped like they do for pets if she keeps on doing this. A fucking GPS implant. Right, as if she'd ever let that happen.

Alex rolled his head from side to side, winced when his joints cracked, then squared his shoulders. "Okay, thanks." He took a deep breath. "Jenner, tell Grayson I want him to greet the arriving guests." The man took off like hellhounds were nipping at his heels. Good. Now, Alex turned his attention back to what was really important to him. "Brute, hunt up Madison and—"

"Aw, Alex..." The big man whined and sounded more like one of Alex's spoiled nephews than the big, bad lion he was. "You know I'm better at *anything* than dealing with females. Maya's different...she doesn't put up with shit, and she's not afraid of me. All the other women act as if I'm gonna eat 'em alive or something."

He narrowed his eyes, and then allowed his commanding power to imbue each of the words he spoke. None of his pride would dare deny his wishes, especially when he invoked his abilities. "Find her, Brute. Tell her I want her to help you in getting Maya back here a.s.a.p. I know what you said, but Neal hasn't returned with her, and I want my mate here. Now. Try reaching him on the phone, Brute. I want to know if they've left yet."

Maya had grown close to Madison after her change. If Neal had somehow failed to convince his mate to come home, he was sure that Maddy wouldn't.

"Fine," Brute grumbled, but obeyed his wishes and exited, leaving him with the other men.

"You three," he said, pointing to Deuce, Wyatt, and Harding, "make yourselves useful. Check in with Luca to see if he needs any help with security. If not, you're on kitchen duty." The lions didn't utter a word. Nope, it seemed they knew better than to tangle with him at that very moment. As one, they turned and retreated, but he stopped them with a warning. "Oh... And be careful if you end up assisting Ashley with the food. Luca just mated with her as you know...and even if she's a harmless flirt..." He left the rest unsaid. All lions knew how volatile newly mated males could be, and Luca, for all of his devotion to the pack, was a really big fucker. One who could snap any of the three lions in two.

"Yes, Prime," they chorused as one, and with that, Alex let their ineptness drift from his troubled mind.

He had bigger issues at hand to deal with. Like, if Maya didn't show up soon, who was going to protect him from the persistent come-ons of the tiger pride's leading female?

Shit, fuck, damn, and growl.

* * *

Huh. There was a shit-ton of cars in the driveway. What was the occasion? An itty-bitty, like a barely-there memory, tickled Maya's brain, but she couldn't quite figure out what it was as it flitted out of her mind. Oh, well. Before she had a chance to ask Neal about it, Carly threw Maya's already overwhelmed mind right off the thinking tracks.

"M, I can't believe you dragged me here. This is a private time for you and Alex. Besides, I don't belong here. Rabbits and lions don't exactly play well together. Remember how I was treated by the lion pride the last time I showed up at the house?" Carly whined. "And Neal keeps threatening that he's going to fucking eat me!"

Yeah, sure, Carly. She bet. Rather, Neal was looking at her friend like he was starved, and Carly was an all-you-can-eat buffet. Sexual buffet, Maya thought, quietly chuckling to herself. *I bet he wants to eat you, silly rabbit.* Sighing, she addressed the unwelcomed man in the driver's seat. "Neal. You're not eating Carly in any way, shape, or form, got it?" She thought she heard a whine coming from the stubborn man. Big baby. "Carly, I do remember. But I've implemented a new rule, okay? No lion of mine will lay a finger on you. You'll be fine. Trust me."

But yeah, Maya remembered. Grayson had gotten all growly because he didn't want a rabbit in the house, and her quintet had looked rather hungrily at her friend. Then there were a few of the bitchier females that had given her BFF a hard time and started a cat-rabbit-fight, drawing blood before Carly fled for her life, and Maya instinctively went all bad ass, crouching lion on the aggressors. And she made it known to all that whoever fucks with Carly does so at their own peril... Because, she'd have no problem going all psycho prima on their stupid asses. Hmm...it seemed that she could be overprotective as well, at least, when it came to someone close to her.

It had been fun. Not for her friend, but for Maya, putting those bitches in their places. This whole lioness thing had turned her into a blood-craving psychopath at times.

Maya reassured her friend. "It's fine, Carly. They've all been warned."

Worried expression marring her otherwise pretty face, her friend just shook her head. "*Fine.* If you can live with your very best friend—since the first grade, mind you—getting eaten alive for dinner, well, I suppose."

Maya rolled her eyes. "Drama queen."

"*Bitch*," Carly fired back.

"Puh-leeze. Queen Bitch, remember? I'm preg—" Maya remembered Neal was in the car, so she immediately stopped and corrected herself. "Um... I mean... I'm so hungry for *Prego*. Yeah, that's it. I'm really, really digging me some pasta sauce." There, she didn't accidentally tell one of her guards she was pregnant, not before she told Alex.

Go Team Preggers!

And telling Carly didn't count. Because, according to Maya, there was a rule in the "Best Friend Handbook" that covered that. So, Maya was fairly certain she was in the clear. Alex would be the first *male* she told. *Right.* That was all that mattered.

Neal parked the SUV in front of the house and shut it off. The minute the engine quieted, Maya was on the move, tromping up the walkway steps, and to what would certainly be the lecture of all lectures. "Come on, chickie," Maya called out to her friend. "Let me get my ass chewed out by the prime, and then we can hit up Amazon for some—"

Maya was interrupted by the bright red front door (because everyone just had to have a red door at some point in their lives) flying open, where a frantic Madison greeted her. "Oh, thank god, Maya."

In a split second, Maya was hugged tightly by one of her newest and very best lioness friends. She felt the smaller woman shaking, and the scent of fresh blood wafted to her nose.

After she'd accepted her fate as a prima and as Alex's mate, Maya had instantly fallen in love with Maddy, in a strictly platonic, totally non-lesbian kind of way. The timid woman was the little sister she'd never had. Caring, thoughtful, pretty much the sweetest girl she'd ever met.

Growling, Maya wondered why her adoptive family member was sporting a cut on her arm. She separated herself from the tiny woman and looked her over from head-to-toe, trying to see if her friend had any other injuries.

"*What* happened?"

Madison stared ahead and clenched her jaw, with her back ramrod straight. "Nothing. Really. I'm just glad you're home now. Alex was worried sick about you."

Maya knew Maddy was lying. Maya had been working with her on not being such a pushover. Being the kindest, the most compassionate, but also the physically weakest member of the pride didn't mean anyone could treat her like shit. And Maya wouldn't stand for it. Right or wrong, she protected Maddy as if she were her kid sister. "Please...forget about it."

Maya was ready to shred a bit of fur to prove her point if need be. When it came to her lions, especially Madison, she was overly protective. *Sound like someone else you know, Maya? Like Alex, perhaps? Shut up, you!* Maya blamed the reason for talking to herself on the stress of her recently learned pregnancy.

"Who did this to you, Maddy?" Her friend stilled, quieted.

Pregnant Maya was gearing up to kick some furry ass. For real. Could it get any more *dramarific* up in here? *Dramatastic? Dramaboombastic?* She found it difficult to figure out which term she preferred to explain her eventful day.

Maya glanced at Carly. Her friend nodded, assuring her with unspoken words that she had Maya's back. She just hoped that her friend could be as fierce as the times she'd seen the rabbit nibble the fuck out of heads of lettuce and dandelions. The low growl she heard from Neal told her that he was game as well. Besides, it was his job to protect her. Still, she was moved by his thoughtfulness.

Maya gently pushed past Madison and cautiously strode into her home, steeling herself to the idea that she was gonna have to *whoop* some shifter ass. All Maddy had to do was give her a name—or names—and point the cowardly bullies out to her. She knew Maddy well enough to know that whatever happened could not have been instigated by her easygoing friend.

It didn't take long before the unfamiliar scents assaulted her. The musky, sweet aroma of random shifters surrounded her, and she heard voices coming from the living area. Without hesitation, she trudged in that direction, kicking off her shoes as she pressed on. No need to get her great, big, lion-y paws stuck in her pretties. And hey, look! No dents in the walls this time around. The same couldn't be said for what had happened at Carly's place. *Oops. Sorry, chickie.*

Shifting would be her last resort, she reminded herself. Diplomacy first. Right. And Santa was real.

Hormones raging, Maya said a big "Fuck you" to political correctness.

She turned the corner and stopped to take in the scene before her. To the left, a handful of men she didn't recognize stood in a line and glared across the room at Alex. But since her mate tended to piss people off on a regular basis, this didn't really surprise her. Grrr... Regardless of who they were, she already didn't like them. Because she, and only she, got to glare at the alpha, damn it. Her lions made up the other side of the room, including the members of the infamous quintet, minus Neal, with matching stoic looks displayed on their faces. They've been chewed out by Alex for her actions, no doubt. She'd apologize to them later.

But none of that concerned her right now...

Nope, her only and immediate problem came from the gigantic, cheap-looking-whore-biatch rubbing against her mate. Though, she had to give Alex some credit, because he did look pretty damn uncomfortable around the woman, and he was inching her hands off of his body. Good boy. But, as fast one hand was brushed aside, another took its place just as quickly. If she didn't know any better, Maya would've thought the flirtatious bitch had more than two arms to go around.

She glanced behind her at Madison and remembered she had something else to do before she scratched out the eyes of the woman touching her man. Shifters could scent if someone was already mated, so there was absolutely no reason for the slut to be getting that cozy with her man. Unless that slut had a death wish.

Grrr... *Focus, Maya.* She had to help Madison first. Then, she'd have a nice little chat with the whore getting all personal with her mate. And lastly, she wanted to see if she could be of any service to the cranky-looking men who had shifted their glares from Alex to her...and maybe help them with their attitude adjustment.

"Madison?" She was sure the little lioness could not misinterpret her question.

And her friend did not. "The one drooling all over Alex." Maya swore she heard the little lioness gulp. Maddy added, "It's just a scratch, M. Really."

Hmm. It seemed her adoptive sister was trying to forgive and forget. Too bad for the woman, Maya wasn't going to let her off that easily. Because her moodiness, justifiably so in her mind, had suddenly kicked up a notch...or five.

Heh. What do you know? Now, Maya could take care of two birds with one swipe of her claws. Even better. Yay!

"Right. And why didn't anyone help you?"

"Alex gave strict orders before everyone got here. That we needed to keep the peace. And bloodshed, however slight, would not be tolerated. And you know how much I hate confrontation, M. Besides, we all know what a clean freak you are." Maya would've laughed at Maddy's attempt at a joke, but she had bigger tigers to fry...or something like that.

"*Right*. He did, huh?"

Suddenly, the memory that had tried to poke at her head when they'd arrived earlier, returned. Yup, now she remembered. To her left was the shifter Council, here to congratulate the prime on finding his mate. And she figured they were probably glaring because the guest of the occasion—her—was nowhere to be found. And as for the bitch rubbing on Alex, well, Maya presumed the woman had to be the tigress slut who led the tiger pride. If rumors were true, she came here to try to convince Alex that the two prides should get together for the next Gaian Moon. Apparently, their females were having some difficulty conceiving, and were hoping to share in the potency of her lion pride.

Um...over my dead body, Ms. Tramp.

Regardless of the woman's high position with the tigers, Maya was going to assert her dominance, and teach her slutty highness how to be a proper guest.

Maya was pregnant, hormonal, cranky, and downright furious that:

The bitch would dare touch her man.

The bitch would have the gall to lay a finger on her precious friend.

Everyone, especially the lion males, all stood around and let it happen.

She'd have to talk to Alex about that later, but first...

Arms crossed over her chest, Ms. Preggers stepped into the room and cleared her throat. *Loudly.* As everyone's attention shifted to her, Maya called out, "Alex, darling?"

Her mate stared at her with wide eyes and what she registered as a hint of concern. Yeah, he'd heard the tone in her voice often enough to know she was in one of her moods. The calmer and sweeter she was, typically meant that shit—and lots of it—and the fan were about to bump uglies. "Do step back, my love. I'd hate to get our guest's blood all over your shirt."

With the statement directed at the tiger delegate, the woman focused her attention on Maya, head cocked to the side as if she were looking at someone—or something—insignificant. Like Maya was a harmless, tiny bug.

Hormones still raging, she didn't hesitate to wipe that stupid look off of the whore's face. Maya had already made up her mind that the slut fully deserved what was coming to her. So, without a hesitant bone in her body, she launched herself across the living room—Council be damned.

Like the girl she was, Maya went straight for the woman's long, blonde locks. She fisted the tigress' hair with both hands and yanked her away from Alex, then threw her to the ground before straddling the thin woman, her arms pinned in place by Maya's knees. The tigress couldn't weigh more than 110 pounds, and unlucky for her, the lioness was much heavier than the toothpick-sized bitch. By like…a lot of a lot.

One hand still firmly wrapped in the chick's hair, she made sure the tigress could see the slow but deliberate shift of her hand. While hunting or when she was surrounded by blood from a kill, Maya typically didn't have a shred of control over her she-cat.

At this very moment though, the lioness within was all about cooperation.

Each finger changed, first one, and then another, in sequence from thumb to pinky, until razor-sharp nails tipped her fingers, primed and ready to slice through the tigress' delicate-looking skin.

"Madison?" Maya called to her friend.

From the corner of her eye, she watched the timid lioness inch forward, the other lions of her pride giving way, allowing her friend to pass.

"She pushed me aside when I answered the door and scratched my arm. Her claws were out," Maddy replied. Maya listened as her friend spoke, but she didn't dare let her attention divert from the tigress.

"Hmm..." Maya brought her index finger to the neckline of the woman's dress, and slipped it beneath the seam at the shoulder. Her knife-like nail sliced through the fabric like butter, until the pale skin of the tigress' arm was fully revealed.

"Now, I'm thinking that 'Lions Rule, Tigers Drool' carved right here would be just perfect. How 'bout you?" Maya kidded. Rather caustically, but still, all she wanted to do was teach the skinny bitch a lesson.

After a sincere apology offered to her friend Madison, Maya let the woman up when she was certain that the tigress fully understood that she and her lions weren't to be fucked with. Not needing the aid of Carly or Neal, Maya was rather proud of herself. Not in an arrogant way, no. But, being that she was a newly turned prima, it was comforting for her to know that she could protect her own.

* * *

Thank god the Council had quietly retreated the moment Maya had finished dealing with the shameless tigress.

Unfortunately, it had come at the cost of hearing an earful from her mate.

Alex could be such a meanie.

She loved him, but still a meanie. Oddly enough, she thought that of him whenever she didn't get her way. Hmm...odd indeed.

To make up for her outburst, Alex had asked Maya to graciously invite the Council to dinner tomorrow night. Stupid meanie-poopie-head.

After the rest of her "guests" left, she relieved her quintet of their duties for the night, but not before she asked Neal to drive her BFF home. She actually felt kinda guilty for dragging the rabbit shifter to her place full of lions, and made a mental note to do something special for her friend at a later time.

She waited until the remaining lions retreated into the outer parts of her home to address her mate with the bombshell news she wanted to get off of her chest.

She certainly didn't need an audience for her personal announcement.

Maya led her man up the stairs and straight to their bedroom. She could sense the need in him, the unspoken desire beating just beneath his skin. The adrenaline from her encounter still raced through her blood, and she imagined that Alex was feeling something similar.

Fighting, to whatever degree, got her alpha male hot, no two ways about it.

Maya scented his arousal, the gentle musk that emanated from his pores, wrapping around her like a warm blanket of heated desire. Her lioness purred in response, suddenly more interested in licking him from head-to-toe than ripping him apart for the whole surprise pregnancy thing.

Just barely over the threshold of their room, she was startled by the loud thud of the door being slammed shut, the wood creaking something awful under the force of her mate's beastly strength. Another step forward and his claws sliced through the straps of her dress, the fabric sliding from her body with ease and pooling at her feet, leaving her clad in only her bra and panties.

Excitement pulsed and pounded through her veins, and she and her lioness were both more than ready for whatever their mate desired.

Between one blink of her eyes and the next, Alex's body covered her from shoulder-to-ankle, his solid weight holding the front part of her body flush against one of their bedroom walls, his large hands already sweeping over the backside of her half-naked body.

"Maya..." he began, his hot breath fanning her bared neck. The scent of wood, rain, and desire surrounded her, warming her skin and heightening her senses. He settled his teeth on her shoulder, sharp edges raking over the vulnerable flesh, but not yet sinking through the delicate surface. She couldn't suppress the shiver of arousal that shot through her, or the flood of need that engulfed her, daring her to succumb to her man so he could ravish her. She was quickly losing the strength in her legs, and without the support of her mate's body securing her in place, she was sure she would tumble to the ground.

His bite was her kryptonite. She whimpered and twitched when he sank his teeth into the bared flesh where her shoulder met her neck, and the she-cat was desperate to be possessed, to be forcefully taken by her mate.

Alex clamped down, just a fraction, and then released his hold, laving the abused area to ease the sting, just as he always did. "My fierce, sweet mate."

She strained to get closer to him, frantic for his touch, but he didn't relent, and pinning her body with his, he didn't grant her an inch of wiggle room.

Maya's breasts were captured by the unmoving wall, her covered nipples hardening as it brushed against the firm surface of the wall. The teased and tormented sensitive bud ached for the pleasurable touch of his warm mouth and skillful hands, the combination of the delicate lace of her bra and the massaging pressure driving her utterly insane.

Alex growled, the erotic, animalistic sound coming from deep within his chest, radiating through her entire being. "Be still, my love."

Her pussy throbbed at the order, growing heavy with desire, longing to be filled by Alex's enormous cock. She wanted to be possessed by him, to have him dominate her in every way possible. By beast, by man, she could hardly wait.

A single tooth, likely one of his canines, scraped along her jaw and traveled down the side of her neck, settling where he had bitten her earlier. He was marking her—scenting and announcing his ownership of her body.

Her lioness craved his display of dominance and possessiveness, and Maya had to admit, she was all for it as well. Sex was so amazingly hot whenever he got all growly and aggressive.

Cool air wafted over the juncture of her thighs, chilling her moist, panty-clad flesh, causing countless goose bumps to form across her skin. Eager to be filled by her man, she tilted her hips and pushed her ass back against his crotch, whining her near-silent plea when she felt his hardness press between her cheeks.

Her silk panties and his slacks separated them, but still, she could easily feel the heat of his erection through the layers of fabric. She had no doubt that he wanted her just as much as she wanted him.

"Alex...my mate..."

With a deep moan, he moved his arms and grabbed ahold of hers, shoving her hands above her head and securing her wrists with one of his brawny hands. His other one disappeared from her line of sight and she felt a hard tug of her panties against her hips. The ripping of cloth was quickly followed by the tinkling of his belt buckle and the sound of his zipper opening. Her panties slid along her skin and fell to the ground, leaving her naked from the waist down.

She pushed her ass out in search of his cock, and let out a moan of pure delight when she found it, the scalding thickness of his raging hard-on pressing along the crack of her ass sending a flare of indescribable pleasure through her pussy. He flexed his hips, sliding his engorged shaft between her butt cheeks, slipping along the crevasse, teasing them both with measured movements. Slow and steady, up and down...

Each thrust and retreat was punctuated with a deep growl, the animalistic sound emanating from his very soul, enveloping her in his carnal desire.

His free hand settled on her hip, sharp claws digging into her flesh and breaking skin, the scent of fresh blood hitting the room, making her even hotter, needier.

"*Yesss...*" she hissed, the sting of pleasure-pain beckoning her she-cat closer to the surface. The feline purred, yearning to be mounted by her mate.

His deadly claws traveled upward from her hip, along her ribcage, and settled on her lace-covered breast, kneading her abundant flesh and plucking at her hardened nub through the barely-there fabric. Two fingers pinched the awakened flesh, teased and tormented her, tugging at it in time with each flex of his hips.

He scratched her vulnerable neck with his teeth, massaging her breasts while he rubbed his blood-filled cock between the crack of her ass. Her nerves alighted, her heightened senses worked to arouse her even further.

Maya's pussy was moist, and growing wetter by the passing second, clenching on air, silently begging to be stuffed by her mate. "Please, Alex..."

Another rending of cloth and her breasts came free of their confines, his heated palm quickly returning to caress her plump flesh.

"Tell me what you need, mate." His hand abandoned her breasts and she whimpered at the loss, but she purred when his palm traveled over her goose bump-riddled skin, sliding along the center of her chest and down her rounded stomach, settling just above the neediest part of her body.

His claws retracted, Alex traced tiny circles above her pussy with his fingers, then dipped a single digit down to tease the very top of her moistened slit. Gently sliding his finger over the delicate area, he then slipped it between her lower lips, toying with her heat like only he knew how. Up and down, in and out, over and again he pleasured her. Maya's breathing came in rapid pants while he kept his finger fucking tempo slow, flirting with her nerves as she patiently waited for what she desired most.

"Do you crave my touch? Do you need me...here?" He sank his finger a little deeper still, brushing against her G-spot for the briefest of moments before withdrawing to tease her swelling clit.

"Alex, please!" she sobbed, rocking her luscious ass hard against his crotch.

"Please what, Maya, my prima?" He slipped his thick digit between her pussy lips again, pad of his calloused finger skimming the concentration of nerves with a gentle touch, and then he was back to tormenting the top of her slit once again.

She whimpered—the lioness within just as desperate for him as her human side. "You, Alex. I need you."

Growling, more beast than man, Alex released her hands long enough to spin her around, before pinning her once again with his hard body. Now face-to-face with her mate, she sensed his lion pacing just beneath his skin. Alex's eyes had turned a deep gold, showing her that he was cautiously walking the thin line between cat and man.

His warm, hard cock jutted from the juncture of his thighs, and trapped between their bodies, it pulsed against her stomach, wetting her skin with his pre-cum. She wanted him, longed to have him deep inside her and reaffirm their special bond, to erase the stench of that tigress whore completely off of her man.

Maya lifted her leg and placed it on Alex's hip, pulling him close. She couldn't dominate him in her position, but she could certainly demand.

"Maya…"

"Mine!" She bit off the possessive word, then leaned forward and captured him in a passionate kiss, nipping and biting his lower lip, drawing some of his addictive blood into her mouth. The sweet flavor of him burst over her taste buds, causing her to moan like the needy lioness she was. Alex didn't let her have her way for very long. No, he took control of their kiss and returned her passion in spades.

A flicker of pain emanated from her wrists, the prick of her skin by his reemerged claws bringing more of her bloody scent into their room. Another growl, deeper than before, traveled from her mate and through her, the vibrations only adding to her level of excitement.

Continuing to kiss, Maya was lost in his embrace, fully engulfed in his passion, his tongue taunting her as it mimicked what he had in store for her needy pussy. He sucked and probed, savagely dominating her with an unbridled ease.

While he conquered her mouth, he cupped her breasts in his large, rough palms, and kneaded her plump flesh. Her nipples further hardened by his touch, she ached for more, and to her delight, Alex didn't disappoint. He captured one sensitive bud between his fingers, pinched and plucked the sensitive nub until she was burning with lust from the inside out.

She rocked her hips against him and spread her legs, her wet pussy opening slightly along the underside of his hardened shaft, the skin-on-skin contact driving her mad. But it wasn't enough…not nearly enough…

Unable to take the teasing anymore, she suddenly ripped her mouth from Alex's, leaving them both panting, and right away, she regretted her decision. Still fighting to calm the sting of her laboring lungs, Maya's fingers started to tingle, the skin stretching taut as her claws extended to match her mate's. The bones of her face shifted beneath the skin, and a throbbing pain pounded from within. Without looking, she knew her lioness was flexing its muscles, anxious to get out and demand that her mate ease her growing need.

He'd gotten her all worked up, and it was his job to satisfy her, damn it.

"Mine." The desperate-sounding word garbled, his fangs descended on her, gleaming in the room's dim light.

Her breath caught in her throat as he sank his teeth into her skin once again. "Yours," she ground out.

He moved his palm away from her breast, and also robbed her of the delicious torment of his dick teasing her lower lips. She whimpered and groaned at the loss, tried desperately to follow his hardness and regain their intimate contact, but her mate didn't relent.

And then, all thoughts deserted her when Alex repositioned his cock, placing the broad head of his dick at her opening, easing it the tiniest bit into her waiting heat.

"Fuck!" Maya cried out.

She met his gaze, watched the emotion and the passion displayed on his face as he slid inside her sopping entrance, inch-by-tantalizing-inch. Like every time before, he stretched her, pussy widening to accommodate his enormous size, her body shuddering as he worked to fill her to the hilt. While they were frantic before, he now seemed to be taking his sweet ass time.

Maya growled, bared her teeth and snarled at the smirk on his face.

"When I say, my sweet, impatient mate."

He could be an asshole sometimes. Her asshole, but still...

Lucky for him, she was kinda into it...for now.

His slow, deliberate penetration continued, until all nine inches of his magnificent cock filled her completely.

Panting, Maya ached with the need to move, to ride her mate until they both came. The pace he set was too slow for her liking but she endured, delighting in the way Alex stuffed her pussy, touching every delicate nerve and bringing them to life. Bursts of ecstasy flowed through her veins, pleasuring every square inch of her curvaceous frame.

Alex withdrew and then thrust forward once again, and she was thankful for the wall at her back. When she gripped his hip tighter with her leg, Alex brought his arm below her knee and placed his palm against the wall, holding it in place as if to ease her burden.

Her mate slid from her heat and then slammed into her, yanking out a gasp from within her chest, the blissful feel of his thick cock eliciting purr after purr from the lioness. Her she-cat approved, loved how good her mate was making her feel all over.

He withdrew and pumped his powerful hips into her once again, the abrupt movement jarring both of their bodies, her big breasts bouncing wildly from the force.

"Yesss..." she hissed.

He did it again and again, increasing the power and pace of his delightful invasion, spurring her building orgasm on.

"God, you feel good, Alex…"

Slam, slam, slam. He continued his heavenly assaults, harder and harder, causing her foot to leave the ground for the briefest of moments.

Alex released her hands and grabbed her other leg, shifting his body to place both of them around his hips, then held her steady before turning his attention back to plowing in and out of her creaming pussy.

Harder and harder and faster and faster he pumped his hips, dragging moan after moan from deep within her, making her feel good from head-to-toe. Her lioness purred as Maya cried out in ecstasy, wondering how long she could go before she would shatter into a million pieces.

Alex fucked her soaking flesh, the skin of their sweat-riddled bodies meeting in loud, thunderous slaps, the wet, lewd sounds of their lovemaking warring with their harsh, ragged breaths.

She clutched at Alex's shoulders, claws shredding his shirt, sinking through the cotton and his skin with a skilled ease.

Sex between shifters was dirty, bloody, and oh-so-glorious.

Snarling, her mate fucked her faster still, pummeling her body with his demanding thrusts, plunging in and out of her pussy with reckless abandonment.

Fierce and hot arousal quickly overtook her, the lioness reveling in the erotic attentions of her mate, purring loudly and growling in utter pleasure. Maya's need continued to grow with each labored breath, with her blissful climax inching closer with each beat of her thudding heart. And she welcomed it with open arms, wanting more than anything for her orgasm to arrive...to envelop her in pure, unadulterated pleasure. She flexed her hips, worked to meet his constant, measured thrusts.

The head of his huge cock stroked her G-spot, over and over again, the rubbing of her bundle of nerves adding waves of sheer joy throughout her already pleasure-filled body. Each and every inch of his shaft touching her slick heat further added to her impending release. She angled her hips so his dick brushed her clit, and the swollen bit of flesh sang with desire.

Her release...it was right there. She could almost touch it...

She slid her hands to his neck, her clawed fingers sinking into his flesh once again, and those golden eyes of his darkened to near black. She knew from experience that he was lost in pleasure, and she imagined her expression mirrored his.

"Alex..." She called his name, a guttural sound that was more growl and demand than anything else.

She tugged on him and brought him closer, urged his head down as she tilted her head to the side. She badly wanted to be reclaimed by her mate, needed just as badly to do the same to him.

Maya's pussy clenched around him, desperately milking his cock as she sought her gathering orgasm. Her legs ached and throbbed from the tight grip of his sharp claws, the scent of blood mingling with the smell of their sex, but all it did was shove her closer to the edge.

"Sweet mate." His growly voice matched hers, the sight of his fully extended fangs serving to drive her need, to further ignite her attraction to this alpha lion of hers.

Both halves of her, human and she-cat, reveled in knowing what they could do to their mate, just how much and how easily they could make him lose self-control.

The slap, slap, slap of their sweaty bodies echoed loudly in the room as he continued to piston in and out of her well-worked pussy, fucking her hard and fast with inhuman speed. So utterly delectable and divine...he was driving her to the brink of insanity from all of the ecstasy afforded by his wonderful lovemaking. Maya succumbed to the pleasure, and let it engulf her in its warmth, all as her well-loved heat began to convulse around him.

She *needed* to come. It was quickly becoming an absolute necessity. The agony of her impending bliss had grown so big that she thought she was going to break the fuck apart...into countless, irreparable pieces. Blinding flashes danced before her eyes, precursors to her looming climax, sparkling lights that were sure to accompany her beautiful release.

She fed off of his passion, the fervid, desperate pace of his thrusts as he sought his own completion.

"I'm close..." Maya wasn't sure he heard, but then, she thought she saw a flicker of passion flash from his eyes as he bared his fangs, and growled at her as he licked her lips.

It wouldn't be much longer, nor would it take much more. No, just a simple nudge over the edge would gift her the pleasure she worked so hard for.

She just...needed a little bit more...

Her pussy clamped down on him, squeezing hard on his thick shaft as he sent her closer and closer to the brink. Another thrust, then another, he gave her what she needed. And her mate always ensured she came before he did.

Always. What a thoughtful lover.

Mouth open wide, breathing heavy, Alex jerked his head forward and struck, before she knew what he intended to do. In a blink, he sunk his sharp teeth into the skin at the juncture of her neck and shoulder, fangs sliding through her flesh like nothing as if it were melted butter. His bite, and the fierce pleasure-pain that immediately followed it, were just enough to send her flying over the threshold.

Maya's body jerked and spasmed, a roar on her lips as she came apart in Alex's arms. Her mate continued the fierce pace of his fucking as she came, seemingly hell-bent on drawing out her ecstasy. She screamed loud and long as pure, unadulterated bliss flowed through her fiery veins, both she and the lioness basking in the molten fire that burned inside her body.

Wave after wave of pleasure crashed over her, submerging her until she was floating inside a pool of absolute joy. And through it all, his thrusts went uninterrupted as she continued to milk his wonderful cock, pussy walls working to draw out her man's release.

Just as one orgasm ended another one rose, another fiery burst of ecstasy setting her nerves ablaze. "Alex!"

His teeth sunk deeper, the furious motion of his hips finally faltering, growing uneven and rough as the seconds passed, and she knew his release was quickly approaching. Wanting to claim him and offer back the same amount of pleasure he gave to her, she sunk her teeth into his flesh, rejoicing in the sweet blood that passed over her tongue. With a deafening roar and a handful of final thrusts he sealed his hips against hers, cock twitching and pulsing deep inside her slick channel. He filled her with his seed, pumping load after hot load of his cum into her quivering sheath. Maya shuddered at the feelings of love that flowed through her already trembling body.

Without warning, a wonderful aftershock shook her, suddenly and unexpectedly, surging through her tired frame.

Well, the good news was that he couldn't get her even *more* pregnant than she already was, if that made any sense.

Panting, working hard to catch her breath, she sifted her fingers through his hair, and gently stroked his lion back from the ledge. He'd reclaimed what was his, and she'd done the same to him, washing away the stench of the tigress in the process.

Seconds ticked by until her lioness fully retreated, quite content, rather sated actually, and now more than ready to take a nap. Maya lightly brushed her face across the side of Alex's, inhaling their combined scents as a hum of contentment built in her throat. "*Mmmate.*"

Slowly, her mate retracted his teeth from her shoulder, and not surprisingly, even that pinch of pain couldn't drag her from her imaginary pool of sexual bliss. He lapped at her wounds and she continued to pet him, sliding her fingers through his wavy hair, letting the silken strands stroke her as much as she stroked him.

With heavy-lidded eyes, Alex raised his head, the harsh lines of his inner lion now gone from his handsome face, and his eyes returning to its pale gold color once again. "Beautiful mate."

She smiled. At least, she thought she did. Honestly, she couldn't feel her face. Or her legs. Or anything, really. A sign that her man did a really good job of loving her.

Alex stepped away from the wall, taking her with him, and walked the two of them toward the bed before turning and flopping onto the soft surface with a grunt.

"Nap time," he said, yawning.

Sprawled atop him, boneless and more than satisfied, she thought she'd go ahead and surprise the shit out of him, uncaring of how bad her timing might be.

She dropped her voice to a bare whisper, her lips grazing his ear as she snuggled closer, trying to get more comfortable. "Alex?"

"Hmm?" Half asleep already, he nuzzled her cheek.

"I'm pregnant." Rather strange, but the anger she'd felt earlier suddenly disappeared with that announcement. Actually, she was kinda excited at the prospect of being a mom.

His body stiffened, unmoving. She couldn't even hear him breathe, or feel the rise and fall of his chest beneath her. Then, he finally replied, "You're lying."

"Nope."

"Tell me you're lying."

She giggled, smiled against his neck. "Uh-uh. Twins, Alex."

"You're—"

This time, she growled, interrupting him. She was really starting to like having an inner lioness. The she-cat had given Maya super powers. And a growly voice to boot. "I'm going to whack you."

Alex leaned up until he was staring into her gaze with a look she'd never seen before. "Truly? Two cubs?"

Unexpected tears began to burn her eyes and she nodded. Apparently, it seemed that being pregnant made her kinda sniffly, too.

He gripped her upper arms and rolled their bodies so he was now positioned above her. "By the way, Maya...you're never leaving my sight again. I'll find something else for the quintet to do. You had me worried silly. And now that you're pregnant..." Overreact much? Suddenly, Alex roared, and Maya was sure the room would collapse around them.

"You fought the tiger representative knowing you were pregnant?"

She figured that that had been a rhetorical question, and assumed he felt that discretion would've been the better part of valor. So, she kept her lips zipped shut.

Maya thought a little redirection was in order. She stroked his rough, whiskered cheek and gazed deep into his angered gaze. Fuck it, she thought. Unzipping her lips, she asked, "Do I get a ring now? If not, I swear they'll bear Josephs as their last name. Not O'Connell."

All the color seemed to drain from his face. "You wouldn't dare."

"Wouldn't I?" She smirked at her panicking mate.

Fucking with—and getting fucked by—Alex for the next six months was going to be lots of fun. And though her pregnancy had initially caught her completely off-guard, deep inside her heart, Maya was certain that becoming a mother would be the best experience of her entire life. And she wouldn't change that precious gift...not for the world.

The End

BALL OF FURRY

Prologue

January

OMG Mate!

Mate, mate.

Carly stiffened in Andrew's arms, her bunny senses going buck wild as she scanned the interior of Honey's Bar & Grill. The members of her warren and the pride were gathered to casually celebrate her best friend's mating to the lion Prime. After getting Maya, her BFF since first grade, through her initial shift, Carly was hanging with them all and having a fun time.

And now she'd found her mate.

Whee!

"Carls?" Andrew's voice was raised so that Carly could hear him over the music. "What's up?"

"Andrew!" She leaned forward to whisper-yell into his ear. More yell than whisper, and a good dose of squee added in. "I found my mate! He's here!"

She couldn't help talking with such excitement. She'd found the male she'd spend the rest of her life with, the man who would father her kits.

Now, she just had to find him.

"Y-y-your mate?" Andrew sputtered.

She pulled back to look at her friend and found his expression...odd. Andrew looked as if he'd been slapped, stomped, spit on, and then someone had kicked his puppy. Well, he didn't have a puppy, but if he did, it'd been whaled on 'til the thing was barely breathing.

"Just now?" He tightened his arms and his grip grew tighter as seconds passed, his hold nearing pain while he focused intently on her. "You're sure?"

"Andrew?"

"Sorry. I thought..." He swallowed hard and released her, sorrow evident in his eyes. "Sorry. Go ahead. Find him."

Carly furrowed her brow. She'd always known that Andrew felt more for her than the love of a friend, but still, his reaction seemed stronger than she'd anticipated. Maybe finding her male now was perfect timing. Hopefully, as she spent time with her new found mate and less with Andrew, his feelings would fade.

Another hint of the musky scent of raindrops and daffodils wafted across her path and she stepped out of her friend's arms. She'd spend some time on Andrew's feelings...later. She needed to find the source of that yumminess. Now.

She wove through the gathering, smiling gently at various members of the warren, and kept an eye on the lions that looked at her like she was dinner. She suppressed a shiver along with the hint of fear that had gathered in her chest. Fear would simply force the cats to chase her and add raw bunny to the menu.

So not a good thing.

Maya had been considered an honorary warren member—hence the bunny attendance—but Carly didn't need to tempt the carnivores.

A tingle of the male's smell crossed her path and she followed it farther. Around and through various groupings she traveled, closer to her goal with every step. The scent of her quarry grew as she neared the bar, and she eyed the gathering of bodies.

Several males lined the long piece of polished wood and she looked them all over. She recognized a couple of rabbits—her cousin Beth among some of the guys, teasing and flirting with them all—and tossed their presence aside. She'd known them since she was little, a kit hopping after her brother. No way could any of them be her male. Which left three others as the likely candidates.

Carly approached, stared at the back of each of them as she strolled past. Surreptitiously she sniffed, leaned close, and gathered their scents, trying not to look too stalker-esque.

The first male smelled as if he had bathed in alcohol with undertones of sadness and fiery woodlands coating him. "Yo! Can I get another, blondie?"

The bartender sent a beer sliding down the bar top. "Here ya go, Ricker. On the house."

The man's name teased the back of her mind, but she couldn't place it. Not that it mattered. Her guy was all early morning rain. Her fave.

Two steps brought her to the next and she repeated the process: a sniff, deep breath, and sunshine wafted over her. Nope. Bunny wasn't having it. She wanted the rainy daffodils, damn it.

Carly knew when to listen. Besides, daffodils were her rabbit crack and she was a lifetime addict.

The third male...she shivered, partly in disgust, partly in excitement.

Damn the process of elimination.

He had black hair and deeply tanned skin. Of course, she'd have been able to see more of him if it hadn't been for the thin blonde draped over his back like a blanket.

He turned on his stool to face the woman and wrapped his arms around her waist, smiling as he hugged her close, a way too sexy dimple on display.

The woman before him stuck out her lower lip with a pout. "You love me, don't you, Neal?"

He leaned close and kissed her, teeth nibbling on the blonde's lower lip. "Of course, darlin'." His hands traveled down to squeeze the lady's ass and nausea gurgled in Carly's stomach. The scent of the woman—human—hit her the barest moment before Neal's scent poured over her skin. Male musk, spring rain, and daffodils.

Her mate, her male, sat before her, his hands on another as he proclaimed his love for her. Oh, god, she was going to be sick.

Carly whimpered and swallowed against the vomit traveling along her throat. She'd been so naïve, so bowled over by the stories her parents had shared over the years. She'd always imagined her mate as a male who'd saved his love (if not his baby-making equipment) for her, and only her. She'd never gifted her heart to anyone, and here he was...

She took a step back and her movement drew his attention. Blue eyes focused on her while his nostrils flared and she watched the knowledge of their connection flow through his body. His muscles tensed and he released the woman's waist, grabbing her wrists and forcing her to let him go.

"Neal?" the blonde whined.

Carly's hurt overrode the rabbit's desire to stay put. Her human heart, inexperienced as it was, felt pretty damned battered. Yeah, she was probably acting like a weeping, weak female, but she didn't care. Without a word to her unclaimed mate, she bolted, no true destination in mind. She just needed to be alone. She wove past the customers, sliding this way and that until she came to a dim hallway. Oh, god, the restrooms. She could hide, gather her courage to face her male. The male who had a human woman in his heart.

Ladies' restroom door in sight, she increased her speed. Yet, two feet from sanctuary, strong arms encircled her, a warm face buried itself against her neck. "Where you goin' darlin'?"

Carly—stupid, innocent, foolish girl—blinked back her tears.

Darlin'...

* * *

April

What Carly wouldn't give to be pregnant with her mate's cubs.

Hell, even one little kit would do.

If her mate was a male worth having, that was.

Maya sat before her, lamenting her pregnancy, whining about the suddenness of it all, and her BFF didn't have a clue that Carly had found her mate.

Because she hadn't told anyone.

Nope, not a soul.

Ever since meeting Neal three months ago, she'd done her damnedest to avoid the male. He belonged to someone else and she refused to claim—or be claimed by—a man who wouldn't look at her, or treat her, like she was the center of his universe.

Yeah, she knew her hopes were more Disney fantasy than real world.

She just didn't give a fuck.

Lost in her thoughts, she wrenched her attention from her situation and rejoined her conversation with Maya.

"By the way, don't answer your phone if it happens to ring, please. I don't want to talk to Alex...or any of his lions right now."

"O...kay..." So her friend didn't want to chat with her mate. Lovely.

"I'm serious, Carly."

Maya had ditched her guards, her quintet, the very second she'd been surprised by the news of her pregnancy and to say she wasn't taking it well was an understatement.

Carly glanced at her freezer, now sans door, and then stared at the dents in her wall, courtesy of Maya kicking her shoes off the moment she sat at the kitchen table. "Fine. But you're totally paying to get that fixed. You know that, right? Oh, and let's not forget about my freezer door, you rageaholic."

The lioness waved a spoon at Carly. "Yeah, yeah. Alex, if I let him live, will have someone come over and patch that shit right up for you. But my visit is about making *me* feel all better, so let's *hop* to it."

"Bitch," Carly fired back, glaring at her BFF.

"Actually, pregnant cats are called *queens*. So Queen Bitch would be more appropriate, I think." She tilted her head to the side. "Yeah. I think I kinda dig that."

Carly rolled her eyes. "Whatever. So we're pregnant, huh?"

"By *we*, you mean *me*, right?" Maya scooped out another hunk of ice cream and downed it, then pointed the empty spoon at her. "'Cause last I knew, you were on a dick boycott. Right?"

Carly stuck out her tongue, then blew raspberries at her. Yeah, she was totally a child. And yeah, since she'd found her mate—but hadn't claimed him—she was on a boycott for the foreseeable future. "Yes. *Anyway...You're* pregnant, freaked about it, and now you're here, and surprisingly, without the company of the quintet." Carly grabbed a spoon for herself before inching close enough to steal a scoop of the gooey goodness that Maya selfishly hoarded. "Speaking of which, I'm thinking about ending the weenie boycott, and I'm totally down with taking one of the fab five off of your hands. I'm thinking Wyatt...or maybe Deuce. Which do you think is better in bed?"

Not really. She just needed someone else to take her mind off the 'tall drink of water' dominating her thoughts. She wouldn't have sex with the guy, she'd just...hell, she didn't know what she needed. She was a great big ball of furry, confused beyotch.

A deep snort, followed quickly by a male grunt, interrupted their fun, their OMG-I'm-pregnant-fest, and without looking, Carly immediately knew who that sound belonged to. Neal had finally found Maya.

Her Neal.

No. He wasn't 'her' anything. He belonged to that blonde...

"I'd say neither will give ya what you need, Ms. *Lucky*." Neal poked his head around the corner. "I'm the man to rock your world." The werelion's eyes were a deeper blue than Carly had ever seen. Soon, the unmistakable scent of arousal and desire filled the small space.

Good for him. He could go to the human woman for satisfaction. The 'Carly Store' was permanently closed.

Maya pointed at the slick-talking cowboy intruder. "Hey...no, Neal. Bad kitty. That was not a very good rabbit's foot joke. And...no cat of mine is allowed to chase my BFF's fluffy tail...unless they've got mating and little kitties on their mind."

Carly forced her heart to still. She hadn't gotten around to revealing her connection to Neal and wasn't about to tell the she-cat now.

Please don't say anything, Neal...Please...Let me joke my way through this.

She glared at her friend. "You take all the fun out of being your friend, you know that?" She snatched the Chunky Monkey from Maya's hands. "Cock blockers don't deserve to eat my ice cream. None for you!" It didn't matter if mating was on her brain—or Neal's—it wasn't happening. Not when he had a chickie on the line, and, based on the handful of times she'd seen him since January, the woman still lingered.

And was still *darlin'*.

Who knew how many others he had in the wings.

Maya tilted her head. "Because of the kind of boycott you've got going on, wouldn't I be a pussy blocker?"

Carly fired back, "That makes absolutely no sense, Maya. Besides, I told you I was thinking about ending it, didn't I?"

Maya raised a brow and opened her mouth, but Neal overrode whatever her friend was about to say. "Why don't we chat about boycotts a little later?" He looked right at Carly and she couldn't fight the blush heating her cheeks. There was possession, want, and need in that single look.

Damn it. Neal turned his attention to Maya. "Prima, Alex is looking for ya."

Well, that ended their fun, and none too soon. The last thing she wanted to do was explore the reason behind the warmth of her cheeks in front of her friend. The friend to whom she hadn't gotten around to revealing the fact that Neal was her mate.

She'd get there...eventually.

Maybe after their first litter...or four. If they ever got there. Yeah.

Swallowing past the lump in her throat, Carly was totally prepared to brush past her mate, walk her friend to the door, and ignore Neal's presence entirely. Unfortunately, she ended up embroiled in whatever the hell was going on in Prima's life.

Apparently, the big, bad she-cat couldn't admit her pregnancy to her mate without her BFF on hand so Carly got hauled along for the ride. Joy.

Hours later at the pride house—after Maya had glared at the visiting council and then carved up the tiger delegate (who happened to be a tigress hitting on Maya's mate)—her BFF still hadn't dropped the P-bomb.

Lovely.

"Okay, y'all can leave." Maya made a shooing motion, her blood crusted hands waving Carly and Neal toward the door. "Nothing to see here. Move along little doggies. Okay, rabbit and lion, but get gone."

Nervous tension thrummed through her veins. She'd ridden to the house with Neal and Maya and now Maya could sure as shit drive her home. She totally wasn't riding back with Ne—

"Neal will take you home."

Oh, god. Kill me now.

A strong, warm arm wrapped around her shoulders, and her mate's scent enveloped her in a soothing fragrance. Carly's rabbit didn't want to turn tail and run. No, she wanted to snuggle in and rub all over him.

Traitorous bitch.

"Come along, darlin'."

Darlin'...

Unable to fight the inevitable, she let the male lead her from the house and to the waiting SUV. He helped her into the passenger seat and then jogged around to the driver's side.

Damn, he was hotness on two legs. He moved like the predator that lived beneath his skin, all smooth steps and barely contained strength. His black locks were stirred by the breeze, and she imagined how soft the strands would be against her fingers. Those blue eyes were bright and glinting as he slid behind the wheel.

He flashed a quick smile and then got them moving, driving over the gravel driveway and onto the street with ease. Thankfully, Carly didn't live far from the pride house, and the trip wouldn't take long.

"So, you gonna tell me why you've avoided me—avoided us—for the last three months?" His drawl was deep and filled with the promise of more pleasure than she could ever imagine; however, a hint of steel edged his words. "It hasn't been easy, Lucky. Why are you doing this to us?"

She squeezed her eyes shut. Her bunny wanted to pounce on him, straddle his hips, and take what she desired while her human half—the bit of her that had grown up on sweet romance novels and happily-ever-after—needed more.

Carly opened her eyes and kept them on the road as the car drew closer to her home. Two more streets, and then she'd be there.

"Darlin'?"

She hated that endearment more than life itself.

One more street.

Then a quick left turn, and her house appeared one block up on the right.

With more bravery than sense, she answered him with a question as they pulled in front of her house. "Tell me, are you still involved with the blonde?"

She placed her hand on the door handle, tugged on it, let the door open a handful of inches, and then returned her gaze to him. She waited to see if he'd lie, if he'd speak the truth, or if he'd give her something in between. And yeah, she admitted to herself, she wanted to look for signs of guilt or remorse, as well.

He frowned at first, as if he had no idea about what she was talking about, and then a dusting of red appeared high on his cheeks. "Well, you see—"

God, life was so fucking hard. "And is she still your darlin'?"

Please say no. Please.

"You don't understand."

Damn those pretty blues. Damn her heart for wanting him and damn her traitorous rabbit for craving him like a drug.

"You're right. I don't." She took a deep breath and forced her body to obey her mind. She pushed the door open and slid from the vehicle. "I'm not going to do this, Neal. Maybe a mating between rabbits and lions isn't the same as if we'd stuck with our own species. I do know that what you're doing with your life—what you're doing with her even after we've found each other—isn't what I want for my kits. So have a good one."

Carly didn't give him a chance to reply. No, she stepped back and pushed the door closed.

"Carly, wa—"

No. She was done waiting. On shaky legs, she raced up the path to her door, let herself in, and then slammed it shut behind her. With trembling fingers, she engaged the locks, and even managed to get the chain in place before the first tear fell.

Damn him.

Damn her rabbit.

Damn her idealistic heart.

Chapter One

July

Little bunny foo foo…hopping through the forest…

Carly wished there were some field mice around…or any kind of rodent, for that matter. They'd at least give her someone to play with and chase around while she hopped the night away.

She wove through the trees, dashing from bush to bush. She paused near her favored tree, tilted her little furry head back, poked up the tiny pink lump that passed for her bunny nose, and scented the air. No other shifters around, thank goodness.

On the night of the semi-annual Gaian Moon, she couldn't ever be too careful. Furballs all over the place were driven to fuck like, er, bunnies, in order produce offspring, and she didn't want to get caught in that trap.

No *siree*, Bob.

Carly hopped a few lengths closer to her favorite clearing and peeked over a fallen log, eyes straining against the darkness to see if predators lurked. Her ears weren't picking up anything, but a wererabbit couldn't ever forget that they looked tasty to just about every inhabitant of the forest, *were* or not.

Sensing no one near, she let the fur fly and raced into the clearing, dancing through the high grasses and dodging rocks. As a human, the area wasn't all that large, but to her rabbit, it might as well have been an ocean.

An ocean that held the tastiest, freshest, bestest dandelions ever. Seriously. It was bunny crack.

Carly ran, soft dew clinging to her fur while she sprinted across the glade and toward her destination. She was the only one of a few in her warren who knew of this place, and she'd worked hard to keep it that way. With so many other wererabbits in the warren, the clearing would have been decimated in no time.

Within moments, the patch of dandelions was in sight and she could feel the saliva gather in her mouth. She couldn't wait to munch on the green stalks and fluffy heads. Two last hops and she pounced like a cat, opened her mouth, and chomped on the nearest weed, sharp teeth sinking through the shoot with ease.

Nom, nom, nom.

First one disappeared, and then another, and another... Four down and she flopped onto her back, belly full and blood singing with the warm and fuzzies that came with eating the greenery.

Bunny crack. Really.

The full moon hung over her, pale light casting shadows around the small meadow. Her ears remained alert, her rabbit constantly on watch for those that would see her as easy prey. The forest remained quiet, the soft song of crickets and the rustle of leaves producing a lulling song.

She sighed.

Her bunny was horny.

Hardcore.

Carly had managed to sate one hunger, but the other was happily rearing its ugly 'let's bang' head.

She hated the damned moon. The whole making babies thing was overrated. She couldn't even begin to count the number of kits born as a result of the Gaian Moon. Sure, she was all for increasing the numbers in the warren. Woo-hoo, bunny power! She just didn't want to help their numbers along until she had a man shackled to her forever and ever, amen.

She sighed. Sorta. Her rabbit wasn't much of a sigher. Didn't really know how.

Anyway. Thoughts of kits always managed to bring her mind—both rabbit and human—back to one man...lion...whatever.

Neal, her very own Texan, tall, long drink of water. Dayum.

The man was six and a half feet of blue eyed, black haired, tanned skin, wide smiling hotness. And the dimple... A shudder of desire raced down her furball spine. That damned dimple made her melt inside, and then she'd get a little horny, and then *his* nostrils would do the flarey thing that meant he could smell her need and then... He'd be all 'Need me to take care of somethin', darlin'?'

In that split second, that single word, she'd feel like a bucket of cold water had flowed over and through her and her arousal would disappear.

Darlin'.

Oh, yeah, she'd be all about 'darlin''. If only she'd be the only one. But that'd be kinda hard, considering *every* woman in the world was treated with the same endearment, the same heavy lidded gaze and slow, sensual smile. Including the blonde, Naomi, who was still in his life. Just about every time she'd seen him in the last six months, the other woman had at his side.

Right. There.

And, supposedly, Carly was his mate.

Yeah. She had it bad. As in, 'mate me now gimme your babies', bad.

But not bad enough to share him.

Sure, mates were supposed to be all 'forever and no one else', but Carly wasn't sure she wanted to test the theory between a rabbit and a lion. Her heart couldn't take being broken into a bajillion pieces.

Of course, all of these downer thoughts hadn't done a thing for her immediate need for a man.

Argh.

She half-rolled over and yanked at another dandelion, tugged it from the earth, and settled on her back, the shaft firmly between her paws. With a happy hum, she nibbled and gnawed, took what little pleasure she could.

The moon, bright and full of promise, teased and taunted her. There was so much she could have... *If only*...

Growling, she tossed aside the last of the stalk and hissed at the great big ball in the sky, ignoring the feeling of loneliness in her heart. Her BFF had mated the lion's alpha—their Prime— six months ago and was happily (and largely) pregnant with twins. What did she have?

Nada...

Okay. Enough.

She sounded like a pansy-assed pussy and she needed to leave that behavior to the cats. She wasn't going to feel sorry for herself any longer, and she sure as hell wasn't going to shy away from the next Gaian Moon.

She was sure that after a lot of coaxing, her rabbit would let her get down and dirty with another male. Maybe.

Resolved and determined to do something different, she closed her eyes with a sigh. She could force her rabbit to accept another's touch...she hoped.

Carly wouldn't risk her heart, not on Neal and his wandering eyes, no matter what her bunny wanted. But she would at least have a go at kits. She hadn't been a fan of not having a Papa Rabbit around as a kid, but maybe it'd be different for her little ones...

Carly opened herself to the night, embraced the gentle rustle of leaves, the trill of birds—which, thankfully, weren't shifters since they didn't have any in Ridgeville—and the soft pad of...

Wait.

Pad?

She laid still, played dead in the night and opened her senses to the forest, scented the wind.

Fuck.

The all too familiar scents of musk, spring rain, and daffodils wafted toward her and those smells only clung to…Neal. Her mate. Her lion.

Fuck, fuck, fuck.

Did I mention fuck?

As a human, she had pretty damned good control over her body. Hell, she hadn't launched herself at him and climbed him like a tree yet, had she?

But now…

The soft crunch of leaves beneath his monstrous paws grew closer with every beat of her heart. Nearer and nearer he came, until the snap and muffled steps surrounded her, his scent enveloped her in a protective bubble.

She'd been well and truly caught.

Carly scrunched her eyes shut. She could play the 'You can't see me!' game. Maybe if she kept her eyes closed, she'd be invisible.

Hey, it worked for her nieces and nephews.

A tingling swirl of magic blanketed her body and the *pop* and *crunch* of a shifter's change echoed through the clearing.

Oh, she really didn't want to see him naked.

Okay, she *wanted* to see him naked, but not while she was naked. Because naked Carly and naked Neal would most likely mean nasty, dirty, make-me-come, naked things. Even if he was still involved with that blonde beyotch.

Yippee! Damn, her control over the furball was swiftly retreating.

No, bad bunny.

With an internal 'harrumph', the rabbit retreated.

Thank goodness.

When the painful sounds of Neal's shift quieted, Carly continued to remain motionless. She was really banking on the whole 'invisible' thing.

"God. Damn. You're beautiful."

Okay, the invisible thing didn't work.

She opened a single eye and found her to-be-claimed mate looming over her, his long black hair hanging in waves and nearly closing them in, protecting them from the world. Even more, he had the dimple out and in full force while his sparkling blue eyes traveled over her from the ends of her ears to her claw-tipped toes and then back again.

"Truly, Lucky. You're the most gorgeous little thing I've ever seen. You're all delicate and cream. Makes me want to pet you until you purr. Would you purr for me?"

Carly, and her inner-furry-whore, melted at his words. Okay, rabbits didn't really purr, but whatever. She'd been the girl with the pretty face her entire life. And every girl in the world knows that 'you've got such a pretty face' is code speak for 'dayum, you're a fat ass'.

For a man, her mate, to compliment her—whether bunny or human—touched her heart the tiniest bit.

Carly opened her other eye, watched as Neal lifted a hand and traced the slope of her nose, and then down her exposed belly. His touch moved to her ears, trailing over the sensitive fur. Then an arm, a leg, his finger gentle as it glided over her rabbit form.

Neal withdrew his finger and she growled at the loss. "Shift for me, Lucky. You know what we are to each other. Lemme see you."

She stilled. Not a breath. Not a blink. She remained utterly motionless.

Okay, so he still acknowledged their mating after all this time. That didn't mean much, though. Not with his love for women and the question of whether a lion-rabbit mating meant the same as a rabbit-rabbit mating. As in, exclusivity and fidelity for all time. She wasn't sure he was even capable...

His eyebrows drew together, a plea in his eyes, and his words were barely a whisper. "Please, Carly? We can just talk. You've been avoiding me for months. There's no one around. Let your guard down, just a little."

There was something in his expression that made her want to trust him. Of course, then she had to raise her head and look down his body, let her eyes travel over every tight dip of his skin stretched over his muscles and right on to the juncture of his thighs.

Hello, hard-on. Like, 'long, thick and ready for a rough ride' kind of hard-on.

She snorted. A delicate bunny snort, but still a snort.

Neal's gaze followed hers and he chuckled. "Ignore it. You've been running from me for six months, Lucky, and I've finally got you alone. Gimme five minutes and, as much as it'll piss off the cat, I'll leave. You know you're suffering just as much as I am and I want to fix whatever's wrong. I can't do that if I don't know what's keeping us apart."

She hated that he was right, hated the fact that a little kernel of hope flared to life in her heart. There were so many 'what ifs' surrounding her, and maybe now was the time to hash it all out. She'd listen to him try and justify the blonde. Maybe she didn't really understand. Or maybe she understood all too well.

Well, she'd hear him out, for better or worse.

Rolling her eyes, she nudged the rabbit to the back of her mind and embraced the magic that enabled her change. Gentle power traveled through her body and the stinging, throbbing pain of her shift enveloped her from head to toe. Too bad the 'gentle' part didn't last all that long.

Fuck, but being a shifter wasn't all werepuppies and roses.

It *hurt*.

As her BFF, Maya, would say, *owie, owie, owie...*

Carly groaned, her voice sliding from rabbit to human while her arms and legs lengthened. She lifted one of her lids, not realizing that she'd closed them, and took in the look of concern coating Neal's features. He'd remained still above her, resting on his hands and knees as she changed beneath him. He didn't touch her skin, didn't pet and stroke her as most humans tried to do.

Nope, shifting hurt enough; 'soothing' someone with gentle caresses while the change was in progress hurt like a motherfucker.

She panted and shifted on the ground, the mix of grass and dried leaves scraping her sensitive flesh with every *pop* and *crack* of her joints.

Did she mention *owie*?

Eventually (way eventually) it all ended with a shudder, her bones and muscles settling into her reformed skin.

"Whew," she huffed. "I hope you're worth all that." She tried to smile, but things weren't quite working right yet, so she was pretty sure it came out more like a grimace. No way to tell until all of the feeling returned to her face.

"Oh, Lucky. If I'd known... That looked..."

Huh, smooth talking Neal seemed all tied in knots. She shook her head. "It's not as bad as it looks."

She thought about it for a second, remembered when she'd first seen one of her friends go from human to rabbit and back again. In some respects, the bigger shifters had it easy, as their change was merely reorganization. Two hundred pounds of man made a generally slightly bigger lion. One hundred and twenty-five (okay, one hundred and sixty) pounds of short chubby chick changing down to eight pounds of hoppy fur—chubby chick equals chubby bunny—was a smidge more challenging. The reverse was just as...interesting.

She held up a finger. Hey, her finger worked! "Actually, I lied. It sorta is."

Concern and worry still marred his features and a part of her she didn't want to investigate ached to soothe him. She raised her hands from her sides and stroked his arms, petted his biceps. "It's all good, though. You're right; we need to talk."

She brought her hands to his shoulders and then his neck, stroked the line of his jaw. Neal was all man, all carved lines, and had a fierceness that would make him a good mate and protector for their kits.

Not that she was going to succumb to his charm.

Nope.

Carly needed to take care of her heart because she could really, truly fall in love with the womanizing male.

As she held him, his attention wavered from her face and then down her body, lingering on her breasts, traveling over her rounded stomach and on to the trimmed curls covering her pussy.

She removed one palm from his face and snapped her fingers in front of his eyes. "Hey big guy, eyes up here. It's not polite to stare like you want to gobble me up, and you know it."

Shifters had semi-rules about that sort of thing. Being naked after a shift wasn't an invitation to others.

Nice and slow, his focus retraced his path until he met her gaze once again, and he flashed a big, completely unrepentant grin. "Aw, Lucky, you don't mean it."

"I think I do." She glared at him. Overconfident oaf.

Neal leaned down, closed the distance between their faces, licked his lips as his attention wavered between her eyes and her mouth. Suddenly, changing to talk to him didn't seem like such a good idea anymore. Not at all.

Danger, Carly Thompson, Danger!

"What about talki—"

"Later." His voice was a deep growl that reached out to her inner rabbit.

And then, it was too late.

Neal's lips were soft, delicate, and tentative as he kissed her for the first time. His skin was like the silkiest fur, gentle as he brushed his mouth over hers, teasing her with his ghostlike touch.

Her rabbit, horny bitch that she was, responded. Carly's body tensed, a wave of need creeping through her, stealing into her bloodstream and snatching away her control. With every touch of his lips against hers, her desire grew. Her pussy ached and grew damp, readying for him.

She shouldn't. Definitely shouldn't. Nope. Nu huh.

But then he deepened their connection, stroked her upper lip with his tongue, and she couldn't withhold her response. She gasped and he immediately took advantage, slid his tongue into her and stroked. Carly moved her hands to embrace him once again, gripped his shoulders like a life raft and tugged on him, desperate for more.

Neal. Her Neal. At least for tonight.

Muscles taught with tension flexed and shifted beneath her palms, his smooth skin beckoning her like an invitation to explore.

Her mate did as she silently begged. She widened her legs and he lowered his body over hers, aligned them from head to toe. His cock, thick, hard and long, came to rest at the juncture of her thighs, trapped between their bodies and branding her skin with his heat.

Carly wound her arms around his neck, sifted her hands through his tresses and stroked him, reveled in the textures of his skin and dark strands of his hair. His silken mane drifted through her fingers, danced over her skin.

All the while, his tongue tangled with hers...

Neal truly did taste like spring rain and the freshest daffodils known to bunny kind. He, simply, was her bunny crack, and she never wanted to kick the habit.

Her mate moaned and his hips flexed, sending his cock sliding along her cleft, the shaft rubbing her clit, and an uncontrollable shiver of pleasure raced through her body.

It wasn't just his dick that was rigid. No, his entire body was a study in granite carving, hard, yet beautiful lines, and he touched her with a gentleness she hardly believed.

Carly opened her thighs even farther, gave him more space and welcomed his weight, reveled in the way such a fierce predator could treat her as if she were fine china.

Then it was her turn to moan. He deepened their kiss, took control, and dominated her with his tongue, teeth, and lips. Neal tasted every inch of her mouth, teased her by mimicking what was soon to come, and nipped her lower lip in a hint of their impending mating.

Because she'd let him. Let him sink his canines into the vulnerable flesh of her shoulder, and she would do the same to him. It'd been six months. Six months of want and need and denying her instincts.

What would be would be.

She just prayed her heart could take the beating.

But she didn't have time to worry about the future. Not when his teeth sank into her lip, drew blood, and then that talented tongue laved the stinging hurt.

Her pussy clenched at that, tightened and begged to be filled by him. She was desperate to be stretched by her mate, taken and forced to submit. She craved his possession like her next breath...or a clearing of daffodils.

Daffodils being the more important of the two, of course.

Carly abandoned his hair, fingers sliding through his locks with ease, and stroked his neck, explored the fierce lines of his shoulders. Those delicious hips of his moved again, sent a violent jolt of ecstasy through her. She dug her nails into his flesh, pierced the skin with her partially shifted nails and Neal shuddered, his whole body shaking. She nearly smiled against his lips... Her big, bad lion liked that bit of pain.

His wickedly talented mouth eased away from hers, but she chased him, tongue and lips trying to tempt him back to her. She craved the very taste of him, his essence.

"Neal..."

"Shh... We have all night."

With those whispered words, his lips traveled over her heated skin, peppered whisper-light kisses along her jaw and onto her neck. That evil touch, the one that slunk into every part of her and set her afire, moved onward to her shoulder. He tormented her, then scraped his canines over her skin, threatened to pierce the vulnerable flesh with his fangs and she arched into his touch.

Yes, yes, yes.

Stupid.

But still yes.

"Soon..." His voice was nearly carried away by the gentle breeze.

He traveled south then, lingered over every inch of her skin as if she were a fine wine. His lips and tongue kissed and licked her until he came to her breasts.

God, yes.

Her nipples were rock hard, ready for him to take possession of the pebbled flesh, lave and stroke her. And Neal didn't disappoint. No, he shifted his weight to one arm and pushed up enough to cup her right breast with his free hand, kneaded and tormented her mound, pinched and rolled her nipple. Carly whimpered and arched into his touch, quietly begging for more.

"Neal..."

Okay, not so quietly.

"Hmm..." He didn't say a word. Nope. All she got was that enigmatic hum, but in a split second, she didn't care. No, she couldn't give a damn. Not when he wrapped his lips around her aching nipple, suckled her, nibbled the pearl.

"Yes..." She hissed the word, unable to keep the pleasure from her voice.

He hummed again, the deep vibrations reverberated through her body as he sucked and nipped at the hardened flesh. His hand worked in tandem with his mouth, each pull shooting through her body and encircling her clit, drawing pleasure through her in great gulps.

Carly twitched and tensed, his every move sending shivers of ecstasy along her spine. Her legs shifted of their own accord and all she could do was enjoy his ministrations, let him have his way with her.

Her pussy pulsed, cream gathered at her core and made her heat slick and ready for him. More than ready. Arousal stroked her veins, hopped from nerve to nerve, nudging her pleasure to greater heights with every breath.

She rolled her hips, frantic to have his skin against hers, his cock inside her, caressing her from the inside out. But he'd shifted again.

With a soft *pop*, he released her breast. Cool air wafted over her overheated skin, causing goose bumps to arise.

Carly raised her head and jerked in surprise. There was...something. Something in his gaze that revealed feelings she'd never dreamed of seeing on his face. Not love. No. But it wasn't too far off.

"Need you, Neal."

In a blink, that look disappeared and was replaced with the self-assured, 'sex on two legs' mate she'd come to know. "When I'm ready, Lucky." He leaned down and scraped a canine over her tortured nipple. "When I'm ready."

With a wink, he continued his travels south, lips dancing over her skin and tongue lapping at her wherever he journeyed.

Carly spread her thighs farther, made room for his wide shoulders as he settled between her legs. She raised her head, watched while he got comfortable. The man was on all fours, elbows propped on the ground, leaving his hands free, and those eyes… Those bright blue eyes that were filled with sex, and that little something else, were trained on her pussy, gaze complete focused on the juncture of her thighs.

Neal took a single finger and traced her slit and she whimpered, bit her lip, and flopped back to the ground. Okay, watching was overrated. Especially when she was ready to come with a simple touch.

"Such a pretty pussy, Lucky. Look at what you've been hiding from me." His voice was a deep growl, deeper than she'd ever heard, and she wondered if maybe…

Okay, maybe another look.

She propped herself up on her elbows this time, determined to see everything. One glance at his face revealed a partially shifted Neal. Her mate's features had sharpened, become stronger, cheeks appeared chiseled from granite, and a light dusting of golden fur lined his skin.

"So hot and wet for me. Going to give me a taste, angel? Want you to come on my tongue, Carly. Damn…" Beneath her gaze, his eyes locked on hers, Neal lowered his face, pressed his cheek against her inner thigh and inhaled. Those blues flashed deep gold, changing to match the lion that lurked beneath the surface.

"Watch." His tongue snaked out then, slid easily between her sex lips and teased the sensitive flesh of her pussy.

Carly moaned with that first touch, moaned again when his next lick skated over her clit, then again when he repeated the caress.

"Neal, yes, please."

He rumbled and then purred against her flesh, tongue delving deeper with each pass, stroking and petting her. His touch traveled over her secret place, lapped at her weeping hole, tasted her inner lips, and circled her clit.

The pleasure built, slithered through her from head to toe and gathered around her pussy until she couldn't keep her eyes open any longer. Carly let her head drop back, eyes closed, while she enjoyed his ministrations. He tempted and teased her, laved every inch of her cunt from top to bottom and back again. That lithe tongue seemed to taste her everywhere at once and she simply allowed the waves of pleasure to sweep her away.

At some point, his fingers joined his tongue. A thumb circled her clit while his tongue invaded her hole, slid in and out like a cock and he fucked her with his flexible muscle.

"Yes, god, more, please..." Carly couldn't remain still, couldn't resist the urge to rock against him, take more of whatever he was willing to give.

But then he withdrew, thumb stilled, and she whimpered.

"Look at me, Carly." It took every ounce of strength, but she opened her eyes, raised her head, and focused on him. Her cream glistened around his mouth and coated his chin. "Good girl. Keep those eyes on me now. I want to see what you look like when you come."

"Oh..." It was more of a gasp than a word, and then it turned into a scream of pleasure.

Beneath her gaze, he lowered his head to her pussy, mouth open and tongue visible while he captured her clit between his lips, flicked the bundle of nerves. He yanked a curse from her. At the same moment, two of his fingers, his oh so talented fingers, speared into her cunt, filled and stretched her. He stroked and petted nerves that had long been forgotten.

Oh, they weren't so forgotten any longer.

Neal sucked on her clit, pulled and teased it while he slid his fingers in and out of her molten heat. He repeated the motion, tasting and tormenting her in equal measure. He curled those digits, pads slid over her G-spot and she convulsed around him, her pussy tightening and milking his invasion.

More and more he gave her, each push and pull timed to match her breathing, fingers sliding in and out with ease, her juices easing the way. Her pussy pulsed, a quick squeeze and release, while his mouth never ceased.

"Yes, more, please..."

Neal released her clit with one last lick, but his thumb quickly resumed its place, circled her bundle of nerves in time with his penetration. "Everything you want, Carly...

Keep those eyes one me... Good girl... Want you to come on my hand and then I'll fuck you. You want that, don't you?"

As if he needed to ask.

He pulled his fingers free and replaced the two with three, pushing into her without finesse and stretching her almost to the point of pain. "Don't you?"

Okay, apparently he did need to ask.

"Yes, fuck yes."

Pleasure built then, grew within her with every thrust and retreat, with every rotation of his thumb. She worked with him, rocked her hips in time with his hand, fucked herself on his fingers as if it were his cock.

"God, you're so beautiful."

She moaned, the truth behind his words increasing her pleasure tenfold. Shifting her weight, she cupped her breast, kneaded the fleshy mound, mimicked what he'd done to her only moments ago. Her arousal rose higher with her soft touch.

Carly's climax drew closer, the promised bliss increasing with every passing second, intensifying with her every breath. She was panting now, hips rocking furiously while his fingers pistoned in and out of her hole, the wet squelching sounds of his movements filling the clearing.

"My mate."

She gasped, the truth shoving her closer to climax. Her passion was raising higher and higher still until she felt sure she'd die from it. The molten sensations of bliss inched closer, the fiery pleasure pulsed through her body, crawling into every inch of her soul and grabbing hold with both hands.

God, she was going to come. Cream his hand, scream his name, and embrace the pleasure of his touch.

She increased her pace and Neal followed her, matched her thrust for thrust as she chased her orgasm. It was so close she could nearly taste the pleasure, relish the flavor on her tongue.

His lion's eyes bore into hers, watched her from behind his human skin, stalked her from within, and the cat's presence sent another shudder of ecstasy down her spine. The feline, so fierce and strong, watched her as she neared completion.

Spasms of animalistic need coursed through her veins, the rabbit within reaching eagerly for her lion mate, and Carly went along for the ride. She let the furry bunny out to play, let it show herself through her eyes and meet her mate for the first time.

Neal's eyes flared in recognition and it seemed to spur him on, shoving pleasure at her in waves as he growled and purred. "Mine."

An uncontrollable tremor coursed through pussy.

"Mine."

Her heat clenched on his fingers.

"Mine."

She arched, hips stilled, and he didn't falter, tempo continuing. Her orgasm was there, in sight, and so close she could nearly touch the unknown pleasure. It had never been this good, this overwhelming. Then again, it had never been Neal.

"Mine."

More and more he gave, shoved at her and poured into her body until every breath was accompanied by a shudder that stole her control.

She gasped and writhed yet kept her gaze trained on him. Always on him.

Carly rose higher and higher, closer to the edge, the precipice, the very brink of unadulterated pleasure, and then...

Neal flashed his fangs, his fully distended canines. "Mine."

She came, the ultimate release overtook her in a great sweep, a fierce tornado that she couldn't outrun and his name escaped her lips. She shuddered and moaned, the rhythmic spasms of delicious bliss poured through her like molten lava, burning her from the inside out and branding her as his.

Because she was.

Each swell of rapture was followed by another and then another and then...

She couldn't breathe, couldn't think past the next beat of her heart while he continued his ministrations, his pace never faltering.

"Mine." His single word sent another wave of ecstasy along her spine and he followed with a rough push of his fingers, an increase of pressure on her clit, and she screamed the first word that formed in her mind.

"Yours!"

*

Neal couldn't hold back any longer. Not with the cat on the edge and her little rabbit so close that his lion could sense her just beneath Carly's skin.

With her scream, he didn't hesitate. He left his place between her thighs, crawled up her body, and pushed into her welcoming heat. She surrounded him with her silken wetness, her tight pussy fitting him like a custom made glove.

His.

Pleasure, unknown and untold, embraced him with this first possession, wrapped around his body and sent his eyes rolling into the back of his head.

Oh, god, his mate. His.

She was it for him, the woman made for him and the only one who'd be in his life.

His.

Carly scratched him, hissed at him like a bunny in she-cat clothing and bared her little teeth as if he should be worried about her bite.

Neal flexed his hips, reveled in the pleasure, but also watched the waves of emotion cross his mate's features...the twinges of bliss, the overwhelming arousal...the moment that his cock stroked that perfect spot within her...

"Neal!"

And there it was.

He repeated the move, his body undulating in a gentle wave while he moved in and out of her sleek heat. His cat wanted to stay deep within her, fill her, and never leave the sanctuary of her body.

Neal had to agree.

He plunged in and out, his cock stroking her walls while she clenched around him, milked his shaft with the tremors of her impending orgasm. Oh, she'd come again...and again...and... Well, he had some high hopes for the night.

With any luck, she'd be a fully satisfied and deliriously happy mate come morning.

Neal withdrew and pushed forward, body braced as he hovered above his mate, careful not to crush her. Carly was all wanton curves, lush and seductive in her own way, and now she was his. Well, she would be in the next few minutes, anyway.

Pleasure built in him, his cock throbbed, each retreat and thrust causing another swell of ecstasy to surround him, his cock, his balls. The pressure was growing, breath-by-breath it increased, and he dug his claws into the soft dirt beneath him. He couldn't come. Not yet. They'd come together or he'd die trying.

Just a little longer...

Carly's pussy clenched around him, tightened until he wasn't sure if she'd crush him or not, and he groaned. "Carly…"

She gasped, her cunt tightening around him once again. "Mine." She repeated the word, followed by another spasm. "Mine." Then again. "Mine."

"Yes, Carly. Yours."

Neal's orgasm was nearing, growing with every pulse of her pussy around him. His balls became high and tight, snug against his body while the pleasure of being inside her swelled.

His dick throbbed, pounded, and twitched in time with his heartbeat until he couldn't distinguish one from the other. In and out, over and again.

His breath came in great pants, his lungs heaving while he continued making love to his mate…his mate.

God, he wanted to come. Pour himself into her and sink his teeth into her flesh. She'd be his then. Well and truly his.

Carly shifted beneath him and then her hips were rising to meet his every thrust, their bodies working in tandem to bring them the most pleasure. "Neal… So close."

Thank god.

He lowered his body, rhythm never failing, and scraped the line of her neck, drew his fang along the vulnerable column until he found the spot he'd mark. His place and no one else's.

Her pussy fluttered around him, milked him in vicious waves, and then…

And then her teeth were on his skin, slicing through it like butter and settling deep into the flesh of his shoulder.

Fuck, fuck, fuck…

His orgasm slammed into him then. Shoved him over the edge and the building pleasure of his release poured from him, freed his cum, and he filled his mate. His mate.

With each wave of ecstasy, each shattering ounce of bliss coursing through his veins, Neal pierced Carly's vulnerable flesh, slid his teeth beneath the skin, and claimed her as his.

His.

God, he was a possessive ass. But he didn't really care.

The lion inside roared its approval. They'd chosen a good mate, the perfect mother for their cubs.

Neal's hips continued to shift, his orgasm unending as he nipped and sucked his mark, while Carly did the same to him. Their bodies didn't seem to want to relinquish the tides of pleasure and he rode it, savored every sensation that throbbed through him.

It was Carly who withdrew first, her tiny, razor sharp teeth easing from his shoulder, and a final shuddering wave of pleasure zipped through him as her tongue slid over the wound. With equal care, he released her, treated her battered skin to the same treatment.

Neal slumped, exhausted, sated, and, for once, his damned cat wasn't trying to rip him apart from the inside out. Nope. Not when he'd finally gotten his teeth into Carly and claimed her as his mate.

Damn, but he'd been driving himself crazy over her. He'd practically stalked the rabbit and craved any little tidbits about her life that he could pry from his woman's best friend and the pride's prima, Maya.

It'd been Maya who'd told him about Carly's plan to stay furry for the Gaian Moon and hide in the forest.

Now he had her.

With a deep, heaving breath, he held Carly as he rolled to his back, tugging her with him and tucking her into his side. From shoulder to knee (damn, she was short) he was molded to curve upon curve of her luscious body. He knew she was self-conscious about her weight, but he loved every rounded inch of her. He imagined her swollen with his cubs, maybe a nice little girl kit now and again, and his cock twitched.

He couldn't wait.

Carly's breathing was deep and even; her eyes were closed and her plump lower lip called to him, but he resisted. He'd exhausted her, no doubt.

Instead, he brushed a delicate kiss across her brow and settled in for a nice nap in the glade, his lion ever at the ready in the back of his mind. Nothing would separate him from his mate ever again. Not even Carly.

With a last huff of breath, he let gentle sleep overtake him, his last few words coming out as a sigh. "Thank you, darlin'."

Chapter Two

The hot French vanilla cappuccino slid down Carly's throat, warming her from the inside out, chasing away the chill of the morning. She ached in several delicious places, but even the pleasurable memories of the previous night couldn't banish the hurt and disappointment that had blossomed in her chest.

Darlin'.

She was now mated to a man who was more comfortable beneath a skirt than standing tall. A particular blonde's skirt.

She took another sip, let the soothing sweet taste flow over her taste buds.

The sound of knuckles hitting the wood of her back door cut through the silence of her kitchen. "Carly? Baby? Open the door."

She snorted. 'Baby'? So, she was 'baby' now. At least that was an improvement.

She ignored him. She couldn't deal with him right then. Part of her—the furry bunny part—was overjoyed with the results of last night. Her freakin' rabbit was hopping around in her mind, squeaking and jumping, rolling on her back now and again and just acting like a lovesick fool.

Heh. Love. No, love had nothing to do with a mating. Nope, it was all instinctual, animal attraction. Hearts never came into play. Sure, maybe someday...

Carly heard Neal's deep sigh and forced herself to remain still. The rabbit wanted to comfort her mate, rub all over him, and make him smile.

"Carly—" The ringing of a cell phone cut him off and she forced herself not to listen, afraid she'd hear another 'darlin'. "Hello?" His voice held more than a hint of annoyance.

A fierce pounding on her front door brought Carly to her feet. She could still hear Neal in the back yard, so it wasn't the cowboy out front. She dropped the cup on the table before turning toward the front of the house. Another round of thumping and she increased her pace.

Geez, the visitor was impatient.

At the door, she peeked through one of the windows on each side of the portal and then rushed to let her visitor—no, *visitors*—in.

The very second the door swung wide, she was embraced in a big ole lion hug by her best friend, Maya, and nearly had the life squeezed out of her. Head on Maya's shoulder, she stared at the four men still standing on her porch and raised her eyebrows.

After the Gaian Moon, most shifters were dead to the world for a while. Bumping uglies all night could do that to a body. But here stood four of the randiest men she knew *and* the pride's prima, bright and early. Sure, maybe Maya's mate had taken it easy on her since she was six months pregnant with twins, but from what she'd heard, her BFF's guards were like energizer bunnies—er, lions.

"So, uh..."

The four men shrugged their shoulders.

All righty, then.

When the sounds of sniffles and hiccups reached her ears, Carly figured it might be some hormonal thing and figured she'd focus on soothing the woman.

She wrapped her arms around Maya's shoulders, stroked her back and tried for a bit of levity, teased her friend about her mate. "Hey, it can't be that bad. It's not his fault he's got erectile dysfunction. He's old, right? We'll get him some little blue pills and it'll be all good. We can even order them online without a prescription from Mexico or Canada or something."

Her friend stiffened in her arms.

Gotcha.

Maya shoved her away and held her at arm's length, fire in her eyes. "Ohmagawd. He does *not* have ED. How could you..." She shook her head, narrowed her eyes. "You're just trying to get me to quit crying." She huffed. "Fine. I'm a tad emotional, but I totally have a good reason."

Maya breezed past her and toward the back of her house. Probably to hunt up some ice cream.

Carly really needed to buy stock in Ben & Jerry's. Seriously.

With a grumbled "Come in," she followed Maya's trail down the hallway and found the woman just as she'd suspected: carton of ice cream in hand and feet propped up on one of the chairs.

"Sure, beyotch, make yourself at home."

She waved the spoon at Carly. "Thank you for such a warm welcome." She scooped another mound of the ice cream into her mouth. "And if you'd been through what I'd been through this morning, you'd know that this stuff is totally earned. I even had a reason for crying this time."

Carly raised a brow.

Maya stuck her tongue out. "I did. There was…"

Her words trailed off and Carly figured that she'd just realized that she had Neal camped out in her back yard. Through the walls, she could hear Maya's guards joining her mate out back.

Her mate.

Gah.

But no, God was not being gracious and kind this morning. Nope. She watched as Maya's nostrils flared and her friend took a nice, deep breath.

Oh. Joy.

And in three…two…one…

"You mated!" Maya squealed and raced around the table, arms stretched wide.

Okay, she waddled, but the end was still the same: she was engulfed in a great big lion hug once again, her friend rocking them back and forth in a happy dance.

Carly wasn't all that happy. Mostly. Okay, a little happy, but a little of a lot of sad. Half and half?

Maya released her and then slumped into the seat right next to Carly. "It was last night, right? Why didn't you call? I would have totally woken up for that." She leaned forward and sniffed. "And Neal? Really? I didn't...I had no... But you've been around each other before and..." She waved a hand in the air. "Doesn't matter. You're mated!" Her eyes widened. "We have to plan a party, send out announcements and—"

"No, My. No." Carly shook her head. Determined.

"But..." She poked out her lower lip.

Carly lowered her voice to a whisper, not wanting the guys out back to hear. Neal, in particular. "You know how I feel about Neal. You know..." She swallowed, blinked back the tears. She was acting like a stupid, stupid girl. She'd dreamt of love and mating going hand in hand. Instead, her heart was breaking more and more with each beat. She took a deep breath and let it out slowly. "He called me 'darlin''. When it was over, he called me 'darlin''. Like I was just some... And he still has the blonde hanging around, even after we met and..."

Maya gasped, covered her mouth with her hand and then reached for her, pulled her close. They'd talked about Neal in broad strokes before and she'd always made her feelings abundantly clear. "Oh, Carly. I'm sorry. But, maybe you should give him a chance to expl—" A fierce roar, louder even than the pride's prime had ever released, poured from the backyard and through the kitchen and Maya's face went white. "Oh. They told him. I was trying to stall. I don't feel like crying again so quickly."

Carly's eyes snapped open wide. "Told him what? What's going on?"

Guilt and more than a hint of sadness wiggled its way into Maya's expression. "They..." She licked her lips. "They found... You see... Near Ian's house..."

"Spit it out, My."

"There was a death last night, and it wasn't pretty." A tear slid from the corner of her friend's eye and Carly's heartbeat picked up, racing and nearly bursting from her chest. God, they'd decided to mix with the lions this time around, see if they could improve lion-rabbit relations as well as finagle a few extra babies to strengthen the warren and pride. She prayed a lion hadn't gotten too rough and...

Maya opened her mouth and anything she might have said was cut off by the cracking and breaking of wood as Neal shredded the back door.

Shredded.

What was left of the door barely clung to the hinges while the rest littered the floor.

Her mate stepped past the splinters as if they didn't exist and Carly rose to her feet, fury pumping through her. That was *her* door, damn it. He couldn't just go around—

She didn't finish the thought. Couldn't, really. Not when Neal was in front of her in two steps and then his lips covered hers, arms wrapping around her like steel bands and he yanked her toward him until their bodies were aligned from chest to knees.

Neal wasn't gentle with his kiss; he was ruthless. He forced her lips apart and his tongue invaded her, sweeping in to trace every inch of her mouth. He lapped at her, sliding the supple muscle in and out, mimicking the movement of their bodies from hours before.

Carly responded, rabbit forcing her to welcome her mate, and she tangled with him, tasted and drew in his essence, proved that she could give as good as she got and then some.

Then, just as quickly as it had begun, it ended. He ripped his mouth from hers, the pounding of her heart thumping through her abused lips. He cupped her skull and pressed it against his chest, rested his chin on the top of her head. His hands stroked her back, fingers tracing her spine, and, slowly, her pulse slowed.

Distantly, she heard her friend speak, but she was too dazed by his sensual attack to catch it all.

"...you told him...mated...he deserved...gutted...looks just like her...family..."

Things did not sound well in the furry world.

Carly squirmed against him until she could raise her head and take in the rest of the room. "Would everyone like to share with the rest of the class?"

Five sets of eyes focused on her and she was sure that a look at Neal would reveal that he was intent on her, as well.

But it was Maya who spoke up first. "They found your cousin Beth this morning between your glade and your brother's house. She'd been..." Tears glistened in her friend's eyes and she took a deep breath before continuing. "She'd been killed while in her fur."

"That's why Ian called so early this morning... He told me to stay put and not let anyone in and..." Carly's mind traveled back to just before dawn, Ian's frantic and anger-tinged voice as he bit off orders. She'd recognized his tone, the barely suppressed fury. Since her brother tended to run hot, she hadn't thought much of his attitude. She even paused for a handful of seconds after his call and pondered listening to his orders, but quickly tossed the idea aside. After her cappuccino, she'd planned on making her way to Maya to talk things through about her mating, yet...

She took a deep breath, unwilling to break down and cry before she knew it all. "You're sure it was Beth?"

At the five nods, she squeezed her eyes shut. God, Beth. She'd been the sweetest, kindest woman Carly had ever known. They'd grown up together, side by side. While Carly's brother, Ian, was the warren's Buck and ruled the rabbits of Ridgeville, Beth's brother, Devlin, had been Ian's Second. They were two peas in a pod and even looked almost identical when shifted. Their brothers had always called them twins and they'd spent every minute together when they'd been kits, with human Maya not far behind.

And now she was gone.

"Why? What happened?"

"Guys? Give us a minute?" Neal's deep baritone surrounded her, enveloped her in soothing comfort. Damn it, she didn't want to lean on him. This was Maya's territory, not his.

Too bad her heart wasn't down with that thought. Nope, her heart wanted him to snuggle her close and never let her go. Wanted him to help her get through whatever was to come.

Maya and her guards filed past them. Maya's fingers stroked her lower back as she slid by. "I'll be here, I won't leave you and..."

Neal interrupted her. "I've got her, Prima. Why don't you have the guys take you home? I'm sure Prime would like you by his side."

Oh, yeah, that'd go over well with Maya. "I'm her best friend—"

"And she's his mate, Prima. Let him take care of her. We'll bring you back later. You need to rest. I'm sure the babies are kicking up a storm, right? Aren't you hungry?" Brute. The man was a god.

Carly heard a deep, threatening growl coming from Maya, but it retreated, growing softer, telling her without looking that her best friend had retreated.

Alone, Neal shuffled around the room and then sat, tugging her onto his lap, cuddling her close, and she absorbed his comfort, drank in his scent, and let his presence wash over her.

"I'm sorry, Carly. So sorry."

"Who did it? Why?" She sniffled, letting the tears flow down her cheeks.

The hand on his back froze for a moment and his heartbeat stuttered. "Ian and Devlin think they may have been after you."

It was her turn to still.

"Why?" She could barely choke out the word. Neal's lips ghosted over her forehead and she accepted his comfort with a soft sigh.

"Because Ian's been having trouble with a couple of different groups. The tigers are pissed at the warren, as are a couple of different flocks. Then there're the mountain lions..."

Carly nodded. It was true. Ian had a knack for getting into arguments. "But did he piss them off enough to kill? For them to try to kill...me?"

He squeezed her tight and spoke against her temple. "One or two of them, maybe. Most of them are trying to find a place in Ridgeville, and while Prime has his fingers deep in the town government and is powerful in his own right..."

She nodded. "Ian owns damn near everything. He may not tear into flesh like you carnivores, but he's a bloodthirsty leader. No one can move in without securing housing, and he has very rich friends who own a hell of a lot of real estate. Not to mention his personal holdings. They wouldn't sell to shifters without his consent."

"Exactly." Carly felt his smile against her skin.

While the pain of her cousin's death remained fierce, she felt some of the tension release and she began to understand the need for a mate. It wasn't just making babies; it was comfort and caring and lo— No. None of that. Not with a man-whore like Neal.

"You know I won't let anything happen to you, right?" She nodded. He wouldn't. Males were ferociously protective of their females. If he were still breathing, he'd protect her.

"Well," he drawled, "As long as you don't run off in the middle of the night." He rubbed her arm. "What happened, Lucky?" He repositioned her and nuzzled her neck, pushed her top aside and lapped at the healing wound on her shoulder. She hated her body right then. Despised the desire that bloomed.

"I've been waiting to mark you for six months. The second I do, you bolt. I felt like my heart was gonna burst, I was so damned happy, but I've got a feeling you're not."

Neal pulled back, placed a finger beneath her chin and forced her to tilt her head until she was looking right into his eyes. Damn. Those pretty blues were shining with something she didn't want to identify. Nope. Because, if she thought about it, she realized she may have hurt him, may have bruised his heart by disappearing, which meant...which meant there might be something there worth having.

"What went through that gorgeous little head of yours last night?"

She swallowed past the lump in her throat, pushed back all the emotion that threatened to wash over her, grab her, and tug her beneath the vast ocean of battered feelings.

"'Darlin'," she croaked out. "You called me 'darlin''. You call every single woman on earth 'darlin''. And, last night, I was just another 'darlin'' to you. I was just like your blonde bimbo." She wasn't gonna cry. She'd built him up in her head so many times, made him seem like the perfect mate in her imagination, just to have all of it torn to pieces by his wicked smile, the seductive flash of his eyes, and then that single word. Darlin'.

Carly couldn't deny the look of shock that overtook him, the wide eyes and paling of his face. But no denial rushed from his lips, and she took the coward's way out.

She chose that moment to wrench from his arms and flee for the stairs.

On the first step, she sobbed. On the third, the first tear fell. On the seventh, they were coming one after another. At the top, she could hardly see.

Between the loss of Beth and all of the emotions pouring through her from her mating...it was too much.

All of it...just too much.

* * *

After getting summarily dismissed by his mate—his mate, for fuck's sake—Neal left Carly in her bedroom, sniffles echoing through the door. Damn, but his heart nearly broke at the evidence of her crying. He'd wanted to stay, hold her close, and soothe all that hurt she had bottled up inside. Hell, the lion wanted to break down the door and take her again, give her pleasure to counteract the pain that had to be pumping through her body.

As Alex liked to say: shit, fuck, damn, and growl.

Instead, he'd left Carly's and headed over to Alex's place. The prime's home was more like a flophouse for pride members than anything else, and he knew he could find some kind of help from the guys. Hell, maybe if he got lucky, he could get advice from Maya. Yeah, Maya had the same thought processes as his Carly (crazy female) and could, hopefully, help him with whatever the hell was going on inside his mate's gorgeous little head.

So that's how he found himself in the middle of the pride house's living room, bottle of Jack in one hand, half-full glass of the amber liquid in the other, and surrounded by the rest of Maya's guard.

He'd gladly have Wyatt, Deuce, Harding, and Brute at his back any day of the week.

That said, he wasn't all that sure about their advice.

"Whatcha need to do is lay down the law." Deuce nodded and took a swig of his beer. "Tell her that she mated ya and now she's stuck. She needs to get over it."

That sounded reasonable, but the man was drinking light beer, so Neal wasn't all that trusting. What self-respecting man—lion—drank *light* beer? Besides, Carly was also hurting from Beth's passing, and he wasn't all that sure that 'the law' would go over well.

Wyatt threw an empty can at Deuce, hitting the man in the head. Neal snickered. "Shaddup, asshole. What do you know about women and mating?" The man turned his attention to Neal, all kinds of seriousness in his gaze. "Seduce her, man. Get in nice and close and keep her in your bed until she's too tired to crawl away."

Well, now, Neal could get behind that idea. Based on the twitch of his cock, yeah, his dick was on board as well. Oh, yeah. She'd been all sweet curves, gentle dips, and he wanted to explore every inch of her again. Wanted to lick her from head to toe, savor the taste of her skin, lap at her tasty puss—

Harding interrupted his thoughts. "Do you want to get him neutered?" A pillow went flying across the room. "Now, Nealy boy, whatcha want to do is—"

Brute cut him off. "Whatcha want to do is hightail it back to your mate's house and figure out what the fuck you did wrong and fix it. Seducing and tricking aren't your answer, and you sure as shit ain't establishing a lasting relationship if all you've got is sex. "

Brute was their leader, the biggest guy in the pride. Meanest, too. But all that was tempered by an intelligence and gentle nature that confounded the team. While he, Harding, Wyatt, and Deuce were ready to shred anyone who came close to hurting Maya, Brute was all about handling things peacefully. It really put a damper on their fun.

"What makes you think I did anything wrong? She was fully *satisfied* when we were done and I snuggled her close. Did all the right things. And then she locked me out!" He downed the rest of the Jack in his glass and savored the burn. "Her mate." He grumbled. "I know I need to be sensitive. She's torn up about Beth, but I want to be there for her, guys. She's..."

He wasn't going to reveal those few seconds when she'd admitted the truth about his endearment, but...fuck if he understood what she was thinkin'. Ladies liked it when he was all sugar.

Neal sighed and dropped his head against the back of the sofa, stared at the popcorn ceiling. When all was said and done, Carly was his life. Period. Full stop. And she didn't want anything to do with him. Sure, she'd been all sweetness in his arms, but then... Fuck. His cat was clawing at his insides, growling, snarling even. The fucker wanted their mate. Now.

"I dunno what to do, guys."

The soft patter of Maya's footsteps against the tile approached them. He knew her steps better than the team's. It was his job. Plus, he liked the firecracker prima. She'd breathed new life into the pride and had driven Alex batshit crazy, which was the best gift ever.

"Dunno what to do about what?" From the corner of his eye, he watched her waddle into the room, her large, pregnant belly leading the way. Maya plopped down onto the couch next to him, then propped her feet on the coffee table with a sigh.

"Carly." He refilled his glass and raised it to his lips, only to have it snatched away by the woman at his side. Maya wasn't much for mid-day drinking. "She kicked me out. Won't let me near her. Woman did a damned ding-dong-ditch on my ass last night."

"You're here to get advice about Carly? You're here talking to this bunch of un-mated dumbasses about my best friend in the whole wide world since first grade?" The guys all grumbled, but quieted when her glare circled the room. "Y'all are dumbasses when it comes to this and you know it." Maya sighed and turned her attention back to him. He wasn't all that sure it was a good thing. "Neal..."

The sound of the front door opening and shutting had him looking toward the entrance. Even drunk, he had a responsibility to look after Maya and he needed to know who approached. The rest of the guys did the same.

But it was just Naomi, one of the pride familiars, a woman who made herself 'available' on the night of the Gaian Moon. There was also that thing with her cubs and him being the father—

"Hey darlin'." Neal waved toward the woman and he took in her appearance from head to toe. Shit, how could he have ever thought the slim woman was attractive? Sure, she had perfected a walk that oozed. And, yeah, she painted those lush lips a bright red that had men thinking below the belt, but...

"Nealy!" She purred his name and it grated over his nerves. The nickname insinuated a relationship that no longer existed. Sure, they still had a connection of sorts, but nothing...sexual. At least, not anymore.

Naomi swayed toward him, leaned over the couch, wrapped her arms around his neck, and laid a kiss to his cheek. Probably left a smear of red lipstick on his skin.

And damn if that didn't set his lion to roaring in the back of his head. The cat was not happy. It hated having another woman touching him, and he let it be known that Naomi's attentions were not welcome.

Maya cleared her throat, drawing his attention. He ignored her smirk and the single eyebrow she raised. "You don't see the problem?"

"Uh." Maybe? He wasn't sure he saw what was going on. The cat was clawing at his insides and thinking wasn't at the forefront of his mind.

"Oh, there's a problem with the pride, Prima? Is everything okay?" Naomi's voice filled the brief silence.

Maya didn't say a word. Nope, she just hefted her pregnant ass off the couch and strode toward Brute.

"Alex?" She didn't have to raise her voice too loud, and soon the prime was in the room, nearly out of breath from running. Maya's pregnancy had him on edge. Hardcore. And the male would drop everything if there was a hint that his mate needed him in any way, shape, or form.

At his hurried entrance, everyone turned their attention to the distracted male.

"Maya? What's wro—" A growl reverberated through the room and they all followed his gaze to find their prima perched on Brute's lap. The lion's face was paler than Neal had ever seen, and he wondered what the fuck the woman was playing at. No one touched the prime's mate. No one.

"Isn't Brute a doll?" She ran her fingernails over his head and stroked a single finger along the male's neck. "He's such a sweetheart." Her voice dripped with affection for the larger man, a feline purr in her voice. "He's such a *darlin'*, isn't he?"

Brute tried to ease the woman from his lap. Okay, shove the woman from his lap, but Prima held fast. "You're trying to get me killed, woman!"

Brute was a dead man. And he'd liked him, too.

The words were barely out of Brute's mouth when Alex was at their side, yanking his mate free of the other man's grasp and wrapping her in his arms.

"Mine." The prime snarled and every person in the room lowered their eyes, trying their best to seem small.

"Yes, Prime." Brute's voice was low and calm.

"Now do you see the problem, Neal?"

I was just like your blonde bimbo...

He raised his head long enough to meet Maya's annoyed expression and then Alex's snarl had him focusing on his knees. "Yes, Prima."

'Cause, yeah, he did. Neal was a flirt. Shameless and undiscerning. He loved the ladies, loved making them smile and giggle, making 'em feel pretty. Naw, he didn't take 'em all to bed, but he'd had enough in his lifetime. Including a certain blonde who was still touchy-feely.

There'd been no one since he'd met Carly, but plenty before then. And each and every one of 'em had been his 'darlin".

Exactly as his mate had been last night.

Shit, fuck, damn, and growl.

He was using that curse way too often since he'd met his mate.

Without another word, Alex hauled Maya away and Neal blew out a long, deep breath. The tension in the room immediately receded with their exit. Damn.

Chapter Three

Pounding woke her and she rolled over with a groan. A glance at her clock revealed it was nearing five o'clock, and she realized she'd stayed in bed all day.

Then everything came crashing down.

Fuck, pain hammered through her, Beth's loss still beating her up from the inside out. Even her bunny was subdued, no longer clamoring at her to find her mate and play nice.

She took a deep breath and let it out slowly. She needed to get out of bed and find something to eat. She had the makings for a salad...

Another round of thumping filled her room and she forced herself from the soft haven of her bed. Whoever it was, they weren't going away.

Padding through the house, she tromped down the stairs, wiping sleep from her eyes while she traveled the familiar steps, swaying as she navigated her home. At the bottom, she glanced toward the front door, but quickly realized that the sounds were coming from the back.

Oh. Yeah. Her door.

Well, at least someone had sent over a handyman to fix what Neal had done.

Neal.

Hell, even thoughts of her mate stung. She knew she'd (eventually) have to face him and work things out. Part of her wanted to simply embrace him, hold him close, and take whatever he was willing to give. The other half of her wanted exactly what Maya had with Alex. She craved a Disney happily-ever-after, damn it.

The hammering began again and she headed toward her kitchen, careful to scan for any bits of wood that might have been littering the ground and ready to pierce her feet. But it'd all been swept up and a look at the entry showed a piece of plywood in place. Well, at least there wouldn't be anything crawling through the doorway.

Curious as to her savior from creepy crawlies, she headed over to the small window above the sink and pushed it open, the frame grinding over the wood. A now familiar scent flowed over her. Carly's bunny awoke in a flash, the furball rolling to her feet and purring to high heaven.

Neal.

"Wha—What are you doing here?"

Her mate—gah, her *mate*—looked up from what he was doing and flashed a wide smile. A few more pounds of the hammer against a nail and then he rolled to his feet and headed toward her, a smooth roll of his hips with every step. His cowboy boots thunked on her wood porch.

God had given Neal a double dose of hotness and it just wasn't fair. How was she supposed to resist him, guard her heart against his charm, if all she could think about was getting him naked?

"Hey, Lucky." He stood before her, the screen keeping them separated, and leaned against the house, hands on either side of the window. "Just came to take care of my girl. Alex had someone keeping an eye on the place, but I wanted to make sure that you were closed up tight." Neal focused on her, eyes traveling over her face and she felt like he could look inside her, straight into her soul. She tore her gaze away and heard his sigh and ignored it, not quite ready to accept that maybe her behavior was hurting him, as well. "I'm also here to take my girl out."

She glared at him. "I don't think so. I—"

"You want to get to know me better. See that I'm a one woman man and that I can be the best damned mate in Ridgeville." He smiled, the corner of his lips quirking up just a bit. She hated his smile. Loved it, but hated it just the same. And she didn't want the best mate, she just wanted him all to herself. "I'd say the world, but you know I'll fuck up now and again. If you can settle for me just being the best in town, I promise to do my damnedest to make you happy."

"Neal—"

A vulnerable plea slid across his features. "We're mates, Carly. Let's not throw that away. We're already tied together for life. There's no one else for either of us. Let's give it a go, angel. I can be the mate you deserve."

She melted. Right there. For the big, bad Neal Landry to break down and (almost) beg touched her, and a little of the pain she'd been carrying all day lessened.

Carly nodded. "Okay." She breathed deep. "Yeah. We can do this."

She didn't tack on the 'as pointless as it may be' that she'd been thinking. She'd say 'I told you so' later...as she cried into her ice cream with Maya the first time she caught him whispering 'darlin'' to another woman.

"All right, then. Go get cleaned up and I'll be back in an hour." Neal's smile nearly blinded her and that dimple made her knees weak.

Her mate disappeared from the window and she watched him gather his tools. "Neal, wait. Now? I've gotta... Ian and Devlin..."

The look he gave her was filled with guilt and sadness and he came back to her. "First, I want you to know that I'm taking you out because *I* want to. Second, Ian wants to make sure you're protected until we know what happened with your cousin. He's got calls in to a few resources, but he doesn't have anything concrete yet."

A look passed over his features, something akin to worry and a knowledge he didn't want to share. She bit her tongue and kept the words that burbled inside her at bay. He knew something...and he wasn't sharing.

"Your brother was going to send a guard over," Neal growled, "but I can't stand the idea of another male near you." His bright blue eyes darkened to near navy. "You're mine."

"Yes." She licked her suddenly dry lips. Carly shouldn't be touched by his possessive, Neanderthal behavior. Really. If he was feeling the need to defend his 'territory', then maybe he was just as affected by their mating as her. Maybe...

Neal jerked his head in a quick nod. "Good. We're going to Honey's over near Stratton, where we held that little party for Alex and Maya in January. It was a private party then, but one of the regular bartenders is a hedgehog so the carnivores are used to not munching on little ladies like you. Plus, there won't be a bunch of meddling lions. And even better," He grinned, eyes sparkling. "There's dancing." He leaned close, their lips nearly touching. If not for the screen, she imagined he would have laid a fierce kiss on her. "I want to hold you close again, angel. Even if we've got stuff to work out, you can't deny that you want me." He held up his hand, thumb and forefinger nearly touching. "Just a little."

Carly stuck her tongue out at him and blew a raspberry. "You wish, cat."

She reached up and slammed the window down with a heavy thud, then turned on her heal, Neal's laughter following her through the house.

Cocky lion.

He was right.

But still cocky.

* * *

Neal felt like a fifteen-year-old kid on his first date. His palms were sweaty, his heart beating a mile a minute, and he could hardly catch his breath. A glance out of the corner of his eye revealed that Carly didn't seem to have the same problem.

Nope. His lovely angel was looking as sweet as pie and calmer than the eye of a hurricane.

Hell, she was gorgeous. He didn't deserve her. Not one inch of her luscious body. She was wearing a snug top cut way too low for his liking, revealing her abundant cleavage for one and all. Her body belonged to him. *Him*, damn it. He didn't care that he sounded like a possessive ass. He wanted to lock her up so no other man could look at her, woo her away from him.

She'd paired that tight blouse with an equally close-fitting skirt that landed too many inches above her knees.

The whole damned outfit had him hard in his jeans, dick throbbing and aching to be let free. He wanted to pull over and dive between her thighs, mark her from the inside out.

The lion was in total agreement.

But he had to keep a tight hold on his lust, and his cat. His angel deserved better than a quick fuck on the side of the road. Nope, she deserved to be wooed, wined and dined, seduced and teased. He needed to prove that she wasn't just another 'darlin'' to him. That she was his one and only.

At least, that's what Maya had said. He'd stuck around after her little 'display' with Brute and she'd laid it all out for him. All of it. Good, bad, and downright ugly, and it hadn't taken him long to realize that Prima was one hundred percent right.

He hated being wrong. By the time she'd finished with him, he felt an inch tall and that was being generous.

Neal sensed movement and couldn't help but turn his head and watch his mate cross her legs, left over right, and reveal a wide swath of pure, peaches-n-cream skin. Hot damn.

A loud honk yanked his attention back to driving and he took a deep breath, begging his body to cool and his cock to soften.

"Maybe you should watch the road, cowboy." He could hear the smile in her voice.

"Maybe you shouldn't tease me, Lucky. I'm a hungry cat and you look good enough to eat."

Carly snickered and he grinned. She wasn't cursing him or giving him the cold shoulder. Yet.

The sign for Honey's Bar & Grill came into sight and he easily pulled into the parking lot and slid his truck into a space. Before his mate could move, he reached over and snagged her hand, brought it to his mouth, and brushed a soft kiss across her knuckles. He kept his gaze on her face and inwardly smiled at the soft blush that stole across her cheeks. When he felt her shift to withdraw her hands from his grip, he flipped her hand over and pressed a kiss to the center of her palm.

"Stay put, angel. Lemme come around and help you down."

She narrowed her eyes and compressed her lips into a tight line. He wanted to kiss that frown away again and again. "I—"

"Humor me."

Her blush burned a little brighter and he gave her a wink before hopping from the cab of his truck. Having a vehicle that was high served two purposes: he could go off road, if needed, and his little bit of a mate needed help getting in and out.

Which meant he got to touch her.

In a half-dozen steps, he was at her side, hands on her waist as he helped her from the truck. Of course, he took his time, held her close, and let her body hug his as he eased her feet to the ground. He relished the gentle curves of her figure as she slid along his length and his cock pulsed in his jeans. That sweet heat across her cheeks spread to encompass her face and he couldn't help teasing her. Just a little.

"What's with the blushes, Lucky? Something getting ya hot and bothered."

She stuck her tongue out. "You wish, cowboy."

Neal leaned down and gave her a quick kiss, tongue barely tangling with hers before he pulled away. He whispered against her lips. "You're right, Carly."

Without waiting for a response, he twined his fingers with hers, tugged her along behind him as he strode through the lot and toward the front door. He needed to put some space between them before he laid her down in the bed of his truck and showed her exactly how hot he could make her.

That close, he could smell her arousal, knew she wasn't as unaffected as she appeared and the cat inside him roared with approval. The lion wanted her to crave him as much as he craved her curvy, furry, voluptuous ass.

Yum.

Once inside, Neal looked around and spotted a table with a handful of their friends. This was a date, but he wanted his girl to be comfortable, too. So he led her to a table right next to the few members of the pride he'd chosen to accompany them. Maddy, the pride's Sensitive, and Gina, one of Prima's friends, sat with Wyatt and Deuce. Carly was comfortable with the four of them and they all typically had a good time together.

Halfway to their group, he pulled her close, laid an arm across her shoulder, and nuzzled her neck, making sure to spread a good dose of his scent on her. "Brought you a few folks to make you feel comfortable, Lucky." When he pulled away, she gifted him with a bright smile and pushed to her tiptoes while tugging him down, plump lips pursed. He went easily and accepted her chaste kiss. "Aw, angel. No fair. You shouldn't tease a guy who's on the edge like that."

Carly pulled away, a mischievous spark in her eyes. "Who says I'm teasing, cowboy?"

The little brat danced away from him and he followed her to their table, eyes trained on the seductive sway of her hips, the curve of her heart-shaped ass. He wanted to nibble it, taste every inch, and arouse her until she begged for his cock. He craved having her thighs wrapped around him again, those high heels digging into his ass while she screamed his name.

Yeah, he could be down with some begging. His or hers.

Feet behind her, he heard her high-pitched squeal easily as his mate danced forward to meet the girls, exchanging hugs and murmurs of comfort about Beth's death and exclamations over how pretty they each looked…where they had bought this or that.

He'd given up trying to figure out what the hell women were talking about when it came to clothes.

Neal nodded to the guys and accepted a bottle of beer from Deuce. "This ain't that light shit, is it?"

"Fuck you, cowboy." Deuce glared at him.

He couldn't help it. He smiled wide. "Naw, I've got a mate, thanks."

Neal slumped into a seat and watched his woman chat. He'd have plenty of time to steal Carly's attention later. He held up his drink and tilted it toward his friends. "Thanks for coming, guys."

Wyatt rolled his eyes. "What, like spending time with sweet little Maddy and that sexy Gina is any hardship?"

He was tempted to respond. He agreed with Wyatt, but he kept his mouth shut. Part of his problem was his flirty nature and while he wasn't for changing himself for someone else, he was all about pleasing the woman he'd spend the rest of his life with. Being a little less of a ladies' man wasn't difficult.

Neal looked around the bar and recognized a few familiar faces. Some of the wolves from Stratton, including the Alpha, Max, were scattered throughout the place. Added to them were a handful of lions, a tiger or two, and he couldn't forget the spunky little hedgehog behind the bar.

Of course, God couldn't leave him be. Nope, he just *had* to toss in a bit of shit to make his night hell.

Naomi was sitting at the bar, smiling at a jackal, leaning close and stroking the man's arm. The woman was nothing to him. Well, she was something, but she wasn't a human he'd be toying with any longer.

"Neal?" A soft hand turned his attention from the human woman and he met the worried gaze of his mate.

He slid his arm around Carly's waist, pulling her close. "Hey, angel." He nuzzled her arm. No sense in wasting any opportunity to spread his scent on her skin. "You ready to snag our own table and get something to eat? You need to build up your strength before I dance you across the floor."

Wariness still lingering in her gaze, she nodded. "Sure. I'm just gonna run to the bathroom real quick."

Neal tugged her closer, stroked her spine, and nudged her head down until her mouth was within reach. He brushed a kiss across her lips, lingered for a moment, and traced the seam with his tongue. "Hurry back, Lucky."

*

Lord, she couldn't even pee in peace.

Carly took two steps away from Neal and bumped right into Maddy. The woman was a bundle of sweetness with just an edge of submissiveness that made her want to protect the woman with her bunny power. Which wasn't much, honestly, but it didn't mean she wouldn't try if pressed.

"Hey! Come with me to the bathroom. I hate going alone."

Powerless to stop her, Carly was tugged along by the woman and toward the back of the bar, along the (now infamous) hallway, and into the bathroom.

Madison hadn't said a word, not during their trudge through the throng or when they entered the small restroom. But the timid woman *did* peek under the doors shielding the toilets and, seeming to be appeased that they were alone, turned on Carly with a smile she'd never seen on her before.

"Great! We're alone." She grasped Carly's hands in hers. "So how do you feel about being pregnant?"

Okay. That had been unexpected. She didn't know Maddy all that well, but Maya adored the little lioness to distraction and often invited her along on shopping expeditions. She didn't think they'd gotten to the point where private stuff was discussed.

"P-Pr-Pregnant? Me?" She sputtered. Maddy nodded. "I'm not... It's impossible..." Her mind traveled back to the night they'd claimed each other. The Gaian Moon...the one night when furballs were especially fertile. She tugged her hands free of Maddy's hold and covered her lower belly. "Really?"

"Yes." The smaller woman nodded again, all bright smiles and shining eyes.

"But you didn't know about Maya when she got pregnant. How can you be sure—"

Maddy sighed. "Because she was newly changed and I had no idea if what I was picking up from her was because of that or if she truly was pregnant." She held up a hand. "Believe me, I've heard a ton about that from Prima." She traced Carly's arm until her palm rested over hers, the two of them cradling the small life in her womb. "Trust me. You've got a sweet little girl in there. Not sure if she's bunny or lion, but she's strong."

Good god. A girl. Her girl. Neal's girl. *Their* girl.

She paled, the blood deserting her face. "I'm not ready for this, Maddy. He's not... He won't be... I don't think the mating is the same as everyone else's."

Maddy frowned. "Why would you think that? Mating is, well, mating. There are different types when it comes to shifters. But it's still the same...you either are, or you aren't."

Carly shook her head, not willing to hope. The pride's Sensitive had super powers, like sensing things about shifters, easing emotions and sorta reading minds, but she wasn't sure if the position came with super knowledge, too. "No, I'm a rabbit, he's a lion. How can the same things apply? He's a man-whore." Well, it was the truth. "I can't think of touching another man, but what about him?"

"Before you, maybe. He was a total slut." The other woman rolled her eyes. "Since he found you, he hasn't touched anyone else. He hasn't *looked* at anyone else. Lord, woman, be happy you've found a mate. Enjoy every minute." A hint of vulnerability entered Maddy's eyes, but the woman quickly blinked away the emotion and pressed a little harder on Carly's lower stomach, drawing their attention back to her pregnancy. "Now, go share the news with the happy daddy and then take a few minutes to talk to him. He'll tell you the same thing I have."

Daddy. Good god. They were having a little kit. Someone who carried pieces of them both. A sweet little girl to cuddle and hold close. They'd share all of those tender moments, all of their daughter's firsts...

Carly turned toward the door, but it opened before she could reach for the handle, and in strolled the blonde bimbo, Naomi. She was a pride familiar, a human who visited on the Gaian Moon in the hopes of getting pregnant, but that was about it.

The thin woman strolled in, all runway model gorgeous. "Did I hear something about happy news?" she purred, but the look in her eyes belied the smile on her lips. Hatred, pure and hot, bore into Carly. "Oh, darling, I heard about you mating with Neal. Congratulations." That smile turned wicked, almost a sneer. "I'm sure your little one will get along famously with *our* children."

She didn't want to know. Didn't. Really. Because, in her mind, this was his first. The girl was going to be his pride and joy and they'd go through all of the baby stuff together. She was selfish enough to have wanted theirs to be his first. She had conveniently forgotten about the Gaian Moon, the part Naomi played and how close she seemed to be to Neal. Pain snaked through her with every beat of her heart and it hurt to breathe.

"Your children?" She choked out the words.

Yes, Naomi was getting way too much enjoyment out of the situation. Her eyes sparkled with triumph, probably sensing her ache.

"Of course. We have three together. Elijah is three, Carson is two, and Ryan is just over six months. I thought he told you…" The woman waved a dismissing hand. "I suppose it doesn't matter that I got to him first, does it?"

Carly didn't listen any longer. She couldn't. It was stupid and immature and dumb, but she was pissed and hurt and…she wanted to cry. Fuck, but she was naïve. No, she wasn't a virgin. Not by a long shot. Gaian Moons existed for a reason, and she'd participated in her share every year, twice a year. That said, she'd never gotten pregnant. No…this was her first.

Her Disney happily-ever-after was crumbling just a little more. She wasn't ready for this, not when it all hurt so much. She should have dumped her dreams a long time ago and focused on reality.

Carly brushed past Naomi and, once through the door, she leaned against the roughhewn wall, pressing the heel of her hand over her heart. She needed to get a hold on her emotions.

Within a second, Maddy was beside her, speaking softly into her ear. "Calm down, Carly. Deep breaths. It's not good for the baby to get so upset. Don't let Naomi get to you. She's a jealous *human* bitch who wanted Neal to herself, and he's yours." The words surrounded her and she let the Sensitive woman work her magic. If Maddy were a wolf, she'd be labeled an Omega: able to soothe shifters with a word and a touch.

Carly definitely needed some soothing. Like, mad soothing.

"Take another breath. That's it."

She watched Naomi, the smirking beyotch, glide past them and back into the bar.

Maddy stiffened beside her and she felt her heart rate soar once again. "What?"

"Your big, bad lion just caught sight of Naomi and is heading this way. He does not look happy."

She snorted. Couldn't help it. "Probably thinks the cubs are out of the bag and is trying to get a jump on damage control." She growled. "He should have told me. *Fuck.* Someone should have told me." As soon as she got Neal to a nice, private place, she'd go crouching rabbit, hidden 'super sharp teeth that gnaw through his Achilles tendon', bad ass.

Maddy stayed quiet. Smart lioness.

It didn't take long for Neal to get to her side. "What'd she do?"

Carly snickered. "Maybe you should talk about what *you* did...Daddy."

He stilled. "Fuck."

She straightened, tilted her head back until she could look him in the eyes. Tall asshole.

"Yes, that's what you did." She poked him in the chest. "Convenient that we've known each other for six months, mated last night, and you didn't bother to clue me in on the fact that you've got three kids. Interesting, ain't it? At least, I thought so! You stupid ass-licking, butt-sniffing, litter box using asshole!" By the time she finished with her tirade, she'd begun punching him in the chest and he had the good grace to wince and back up with each strike. Not that she hurt him.

More's the pity.

"Carly..." He held his hands up. "I was waiting for the right time."

Carly snapped her teeth at him, wishing that she was more fierce that a just a little fuzzy bunny.

"Like when you first wrapped your arms around me, darlin'? Or when you took me home a few months ago, darlin'? Or when you came to me last night and *claimed* me, darlin'?" Yes, she knew she was probably more emotional because of her pregnancy, but that didn't calm her one bit.

"Any time during all that you could have mentioned cubs. But, no, I had to hear it from *her*." She spat the word, disgusted with even having to mention the skinny bitch. That woman had taken too much joy in announcing the existence of their children. Hurting her on purpose.

Before she could smack him again, he snagged her, hugged her close, and propped his chin on her head. "You're right."

His chest rose and fell with his sigh. "I'm a coward. Totally. You were saving yourself for your mate, fighting the moon, and I've been a slave to it. You were already against me for being a 'man-whore'. I didn't want to add three more reasons for you to resist me even more. And my relationship with Naomi is permanent because of the little ones." His lips brushed across her temple and she refused to melt against him. She wasn't ready to forgive him. Yet. "You still don't really believe I'm your mate. Still think I'm going to be unfaithful." A single large finger tapped at her chin and she raised her face to stare into his. "But you're it for me, Carly. My mate. My world. I sound like a pussy." She wasn't going to snicker. Really. "But I live for your smiles. I love you, baby. You don't have to say it back; just know that I do."

Neal really did take all the fun outta being mad.

Asshole.

And now she felt the sting of tears behind her eyes. With a huff, she thought of something else to be pissed about. "In a bar, Neal? A bar? 'I love you', here?"

He looked over her head and she heard him talking to the forgotten lioness. "Little help here, Maddy?"

The woman giggled and skirted past them. "You're on your own, big guy. But, I will tell ya that she's got a secret of her own. Maybe you should drag her out of here. I have a feeling you'll need a bed. Soon."

Alone. Relatively. Neal tightened his hold in a small hug. "So, gonna tell me?"

She could feel the tension strumming through his veins. "What if I don't wanna?"

"Carly…" She could hear the threatening growl in his voice.

"I won't be threatened by the big, bad lion, cowboy."

"Fine. Please? Pretty please with whipped cream and me lapping at your pretty pussy for hours?"

Carly rolled her eyes. She was annoyed, but her rabbit was definitely interested in the whipped cream.

"Fine." She huffed and put a tiny bit of space between them, stared right into his eyes and said, "I'm pregnant."

*

Pregnant. Hot damn.

Oh. Damn.

Maddy had obviously told Carly about their cub and Naomi had swooped in and chatted about Elijah, Carson, and Ryan right after.

Bitch.

In all honesty, he hadn't followed Carly's tirade all that well, but now he understood everything that she'd screamed at him.

What the hell had he ever seen in the human woman? Sure, the moon had a fierce pull, but he should have tried to resist, should have waited for the woman who was now in his arms. Or, hell, picked a woman worth having.

Without hesitation, he leaned down and kissed Carly, stroking and teasing the seam of her lips until she opened for him and then he chased her taste. His mate was all surrender and sweetness. He savored every hint of her flavor, poured his love into the kiss and prayed that they could move past the confusion and hurt.

His cock throbbed in his jeans, begging to be released, aching to fill his mate. Not that he could get her any more pregnant than she already was, but he could give it the old college try.

Reluctant to release her, he slowed their tangle of tongues and broke the kiss with a last flick to her bottom lip. "Angel, I think Maddy's right. We need to get out of here."

"You're happy, then?" A flush stole over her cheeks.

"More than you could imagine." He cupped her cheek. "Lemme take you home and show you."

"We're gonna have to talk about things."

He winced. Well, damn. He'd really hoped they could just skip over that part. "Yeah, Lucky. We will."

Neal tugged her arms from around his waist and snagged her hand. Without another word, he wove through the bar, his mate right on his heels. A minute later, they pushed through the front door and into the night, the cool air enveloping them, and he took a deep breath, hoping it would dampen his need.

His mate was pregnant.

There was no doubt that he loved each of his children, but his *mate* was carrying his young. Unfamiliar protective instincts poured through him and the lion paced, both thrilled and agitated. It rejoiced in the impending birth, but clawed at the human side of him for bringing their mate out and making her vulnerable. It couldn't protect her in the open, outside of their den.

Their feet crunched on the loose gravel, stones shifting beneath their shoes. The sounds of music lessened as they put distance between them and the building, quiet wrapping around them while they approached his truck.

Just as they reached the bumper of his vehicle, two soft *thunks* split the night air, and Neal recognized the sounds the moment they reached his ears. Someone was firing a gun with a silencer. Close. While the sound wasn't like the crack of an unaltered gun, it was lessened by the modification, but nowhere near as silent as many believed.

He spun on his heels, yanked on Carly, and lowered her to the ground, his body hovering over hers. Another half-dozen shots split the darkness and then the rapid retreat over gravel split the night.

"Carly? Angel?"

His answer was a low moan.

Shit, fuck, damn, and growl.

Chapter Four

"For the love of lettuce! I haven't been shot!" Carly shoved at Neal's hands. The man was bound and determined to keep her in bed and she was just as resolved to get her bubble butt into the living room.

"Carly…" Her mate's voice was low and deep, too low for a human male, and that told her just how close Neal was to losing control.

Taking a deep breath, she reached up and placed her palm against his cheek. The lines of his face were hard, ridges instead of smooth bones. She stroked and petted him, watched while his eyes lost some of his panic.

"Cowboy, I'm fine. I didn't even need stitches. The bullet grazed my arm and the thing is already healed." She growled at him. "Let me out of this bed and let's go talk with the others."

See? She could totally be all diplomatic and shit. She hadn't even bitched about him stripping her down once they'd arrived at his home.

He grumbled and she couldn't quite make out his words. "What?"

Neal gave her a glaring stare. "You're naked. I don't want them looking at you."

Carly rolled her eyes and shoved at his shoulders. "Okay, it's your fault I'm naked, so shaddup about that. And Neal? I'm yours. *Yours.* I don't want those guys, just like you don't want any other women." At least she hoped. "Right?"

"I guess I'll just have to prove to you how much I want you, and only you, won't I?" Oh. That smile was predatory. His eyes seemed to glow in the low light, the right side of his mouth kicked up just enough for a hint of his dimple to appear. His body was too languid now, too smooth moving, and she figured he and lion had come to the conclusion that making love was better than fighting.

Had it been *any* other time, she would have agreed.

As it was, they had three shifter leaders out in Neal's living room, and all that testosterone and power could easily spiral out of control if they didn't get through everything and get them shoved back to their own territories ASAP.

She'd hardly blinked and then his hands were on her, shoving the blanket aside, head bending down to her breast. Neal captured her nipple with his lips and tongued the now hard nub, drawing it into the moist cavern of his mouth.

Her pussy responded in an instant, grew plump and wet, pulsed with every beat of her heart. She panted and arched, gave him more of her.

Neal palmed her neglected breast, kneading and teasing her. With every pull on her nipple, a shudder of arousal slithered through her as if the nub had a direct line to her clit. "Mmm..."

Carly slid her fingers into his hair, pulled him closer. The bunny, that total slut, wanted him, wanted to nibble and bite and kiss him from head to toe. Fuck getting shot at; she craved her mate.

Hopefully, someday, the heat of their new mating would dim. It couldn't be healthy to walk around with this all-consuming need twenty-four seven.

Who was she kidding? She never wanted this desire for him to cool. Ever. She craved the taste of his skin, his blood in her mouth as she sunk her teeth into his shoulder, and the feeling of being filled by him.

He released her breast and blew a soft puff of warm air across the damp flesh. "I almost lost you."

"You didn't almost lose me, idjit."

His talented pink tongue snaked out and flicked her stiff flesh. "Well, if I didn't almost lose you, I guess there's no reason to let the lion have you right now. He's anxious to slide into your heat, Lucky. Wants to make sure you're alive."

Neal's hand drifted down her ribs, over the gentle rounding of her stomach and cupped her needy pussy. She widened her legs without question, anxious for his touch.

He slid a single finger between her sex lips, her wetness allowing him to touch her with ease, and glanced over her clit. She whimpered as a tiny bolt of arousal caused her pussy to clench.

"Okay. You win." That talented digit traveled further south and circled her heat, danced around her hole, and she was desperate to have him inside her. "Need you."

All she got was a wicked smile, his blue eyes deepening and shifting to a dark gold. Oh, his kitty seemed all about this.

Between one heartbeat and the next, her mate was between her thighs, his jeans parted just enough for his thick cock to rise hard and strong from his groin. "Need you, too."

The tip of his cock settled against her wet hole, kissing the entrance to her body and teasing her with what was to come.

Carly rocked her hips, raised them the tiniest bit, and silently begged for his possession.

"Slow, angel." With a huff, she relaxed into the soft surface of his bed. "That's my girl."

Then he moved, gave her what she craved, and filled her.

Sorta.

No, instead of slamming home as he'd done the previous night, he went slow, inched his way into her pussy with infinite care.

Neal gave her an inch and then retreated, gave her two and then withdrew once again. Three and then out...on and on he teased her, gifted her with what she desired, but then took it away.

He possessed her, stretched and speared her on his cock in tortuous increments until she thought she'd go mad with her desire. With each thrust, her pussy pulsed and clenched on his invasion, clit twitching with desperate need, and slivers of pleasure poured through her.

Every pound of her heart and gasping breath teased her.

Carly's nipples drew up tight and hard, the nubs throbbing and practically begging for attention.

Eyes trained on him, she brought her hands to her breasts, stroked and tormented them with her palms, plucked her flesh with her thumb and forefinger, pinched and rolled the sensitive skin.

And still he tortured her. That thick cock, his strong length of silk over steel, penetrated her in gentle, possessive strokes.

"You're beautiful. My angel. My mate." Neal's words came with huffing breaths, sweat coating his chest as he gave her pleasure.

Carly abandoned one breast and settled her hand on the back of his neck, pulled him to her. "My mate." She whispered against his lips. "Claim me, my mate."

That was all the urging he needed. With a deep growl, Neal withdrew from her body, her pussy clinging to his shaft as he pulled from her, and then shoved his way back into her heat, sending the headboard slamming against the wall.

Carly screamed and arched, the pure pleasure of his possession overwhelming the desire to be quiet. No, she couldn't withhold her sounds, not when his cock stroked her from within, scraped over sensitive nerves that ached for his touch. His hipbone pressed against her clit and she reveled in her mate's ownership.

He repeated the move, a quick withdrawal followed by a fierce thrust. The banging of the headboard mingled with their breathless moans and groans while he continued. In and then out, faster and harder with each flex of his muscles.

Neal grunted and heaved over her, chased his pleasure while giving her great doses of her own.

Hand still curved around his neck, she sunk her nails into his flesh, added pain to his ecstasy, and the scent of fresh blood filled the room.

Her mate growled and flashed his elongated fangs at her. "Mine."

She did the same. Not as impressive since she was a rabbit, but still. "Yours."

Neal lowered his head to her chest, pinched the flesh of her breast between his jaws and pierced the vulnerable skin, adding the flavors of her to the fragrance of their sex.

With blood flowing, his pace increased, the thump of the headboard against the wall nearly matching that of their heart rates while he pummeled her with his cock. His entire length pistoned in and out of her wet pussy. Her body accepted him with ease, eagerly clinging to him with every move.

Carly's cunt rippled around him, the thrum of his every stroke stoked her arousal, sent her pleasure spiraling higher with each thrust, each meeting of their flesh. Her clit throbbed and twitched, each brush of his pelvic bone easing her closer to the edge, nearer and nearer to her release.

In her mind, her climb to bliss resembled a cliff, her furry bunny legs bringing her closer and closer to the edge, spurred by her mate's attentions. By then, desire pulsed through her veins, pounded and beat at her, chased her toward the final explosion of her need.

She didn't resist the pull. No, she craved it, was desperate to pulse and burst around her mate, milk his cock and encourage his release to mirror hers and fill her with his cum.

"Mate, mate, mate…" The word became a chant, each word punctuating his thrusts and she kept her gaze focused on his features, watched the look of pleasure and pain ghost across his face. "Come with me, mate."

The words ended on a breathless gasp, but Neal answered her call. His pace increased once again, one thrust after another as he pounded her needy cunt. Over and over.

That cliff, that representation of her orgasm, was suddenly before her, the edge within her grasp. And she embraced it. Carly flung her pleasure-filled body over the threshold and soared through the air, let the sky embrace her, ruffle her delicate fur, and pound along her veins.

Pure bliss—an ecstasy she'd never known—enveloped her, and it blossomed. Her pussy clenched around him in a jerky rhythm, milking his cock while her own release crammed into every corner of her body from head to toe.

She screamed his name and pulled at him, brought his shoulder to her mouth and didn't hesitate to sink her teeth into him. She slipped through his skin and grasped his muscle, clenched and sucked, drank down the essence of her mate.

And still her body twitched and spasmed with the pleasure that pounded through her.

Neal mirrored her movements, his thrusts suddenly jerky and inconsistent, until he sealed his hips against her, cock throbbing and seeming to grow inside her pussy. His dick twitched and pulsed, signaling his release and his teeth were suddenly buried in her flesh, mouth sucking and tongue laving her abused body.

They remained still, locked and tasting each other while their breathing returned to normal.

Minutes—maybe hours—later, she slid her mouth from his battered shoulder and Neal did the same, slumping over her, his cock, now soft, still deep within her pussy.

Okay, hot, dirty, 'OMG I almost lost you' sex was the best evah.

Seriously.

Coated in sweat and smears of blood, Carly relaxed fully into the bed, exhausted. She just wanted to sleep…

Of course, the men waiting in the living room wouldn't let them. The fierce *thump*, *thump*, *thump* of a fist hitting the bedroom door pulled them out of their exhaustion.

"Let's go!" Alex's voice echoed through the room.

With a reluctant groan, Neal rolled away from her. "Come on, angel. Let's get this over with. I want to figure out what the hell is going on." He stroked her arm, caught her hand and brought it to his lips. "I want to get on with our lives and make sure you and our baby are safe."

Resolved, Carly crawled over him and from the bed, tugged Neal along with her, and then hunted for clothes. She found her top, blood staining the fabric, and frowned. "Cowboy? Do you have something else I can wear?"

In a flash, a white button down shirt appeared before her along with a pair of sweatpants. She snatched them and he crowded her toward the wall, pressing her against the hard surface, his erect cock settling between the cheeks of her ass.

"Damn, angel. I want you in my clothes. Want to surround you." He ground his shaft against her heated skin. "Want you..."

"Neal!" Alex barked out her mate's name.

Heh. Barked.

With a snarl, Neal left her, a quick swat to her ass before he moved out of range.

Frowning, she tugged on his clothes, making sure that the buttons were all secured tightly, and then tromped to the bedroom door. Her mate at her side, they headed to the living room, right toward a crowd of carnivores.

And she had blood on her skin.

Lovely.

It wasn't long before Neal was pulling her through his home; she got the impression of dark colors, large furniture, and not much else. The walls were sparse and empty. She'd change all that after she moved in. And she wasn't going to examine that decision all that much. Sure, they still had issues, but after the bite, things had shifted between them. She didn't want to examine the change; she was afraid she'd overthink everything and get them back to where they'd started. For now, she'd enjoy his attention, trust in his professed love, and try very, very hard not to claw out Naomi's eyes.

Okay, somewhat hard.

But if that beyotch...

She took a deep breath. The woman was the mother of Neal's children. She couldn't kill her, no matter how much the bunny wanted the bitch's blood. Her relationship with Neal had turned her into a freakin' carnivore.

Ick.

Okay, only 'ick' if she wanted to murder anyone *but* Naomi.

Carly was pulled from her thoughts of ripping Neal's ex limb from limb when she stepped into the living room and into the lion's den. Or rather, lion slash wolf slash rabbit den.

Seated around the room were the prime and his second, Grayson. Not far from them were Max, Alpha of the Stratton wolves, along with his enforcer, Riley, and then Ian, the warren's Buck, and his second, Devlin. Poor Devlin looked exhausted and wrung out. The normally bright eyed, smiling man was withdrawn, eyes sunken with dark bags just below them. He looked defeated.

Neal tugged her to a large, leather chair nearby and settled into the seat, dragging her to sit on his lap.

"What are we dealing with?" Her mate didn't bother with introductions. "Why's someone after Carly?"

Carly opened her mouth to ask what the fuck was going on, why her mate thought *she* was the target of the nights fun, but Alex cut her off.

He sighed and began. "A quick survey of the parking lot didn't reveal much of anything. We found nine millimeter shell casings along the side of the building, but with so many customers..." The prime shrugged and sighed. "I left Wyatt and Deuce behind to follow a few trails."

"Why do we think someone's after *me*? It could have been someone going after Neal..." Every male in the room looked at her like she was an idiot, including her mate. He was so not getting rabbit pussy anytime soon. "Me?"

She turned her attention to her brother. "Ian?" Carly glanced at Devlin. "Dev?"

Kind, tired eyes met hers and Dev's gravelly voice washed over her. "There was a note with Beth's..." He took a deep breath, closed his eyes for a moment and then continued. "Her body. We won't go into details, but you were the target. It was pretty vague, but they definitely wanted you."

Target.

She swallowed past the lump in her throat. "Beth died for me? And you think today was an attempt on my life?" Tears burned her eyes and a tear slid down her cheek. "Why? I haven't... I'm not involved in the warren or the pride. I'm a nobody."

Ian leaned forward. "You're my sister and Neal's mate, and Neal guards the local pride's prima. With your death, Maya and I would have been devastated. Add in Alex being upset over Maya's being upset... The warren would go into chaos without a leader keeping everyone under control and I doubt I'd be able to do that if I lost you. Neal wouldn't be functional." Carly agreed. Even if they hadn't known one another long, mates could barely live without their other half. "It would then leave Maya vulnerable and Alex would be just as torn up. We'd all be easy prey."

Both Alex and Neal growled, sending the tension in the room skyrocketing.

"Enough." Max, the proverbial big, bad wolf, pulled their attention. "We've got three theories. It's either personal, Freedom, or the HSE."

She was pushing for personal simply because Freedom was a group focused on destroying the warren, pack, pride...whatever relationship between shifters. They were anti-authoritarian. The HSE, Humans for Shifter Extermination, just wanted shifters gone altogether and killed indiscriminately. Killing Carly would meet Freedom's needs... Not so much for HSE. Regardless, both of those options sent a shiver of dread down her spine, fear quickly following that emotion.

And hey, cloaking herself in fear in a room of men who'd like to eat her for dinner was a not good, very bad, thing.

Joy.

Carly cleared her throat and raised her hand. "I vote for personal. Naomi is a total 'psycho hose beast'. She seriously hates me. Like, 'she wouldn't be concerned if I was dead', kind of hate. And, dude, the whole 'hell hath no fury' saying had to come from somewhere, right?"

The men all nodded, but Alex and Grayson didn't look all that convinced. The prime and Neal shared a look she couldn't interpret, but she sure as hell knew it didn't mean anything good. She was seriously going to torture him until she got an explanation.

"We didn't smell a human around Beth and I know Naomi's scent. There were rabbits, of course...a male or two I recognized, but no human." Alex leaned forward, hands clasped loosely between his knees, looking just as tired as she felt. "Besides, she's the mother of Neal's cubs. I doubt she'd hurt him that way. Mates have been known to follow their other halves into death and killing you would mean killing him."

She slumped against Neal. "So that leaves two sets of crazies, both set on causing trouble by killing me." That statement drew another growl from her mate and she stroked his forearm. "Easy cowboy. You're not going to let anything happen to me."

The ring of a phone broke the silence and Riley, Max's enforcer, dug his cell out of his pocket. "Yeah... We sure? Right... No, that's good... I'll pass it along... Give us five." He ended his call, swept the room with his gaze and focused on Alex. "Your boys found something, but need you to check it out. They can't figure out what they're sniffing at." He turned his attention to his Alpha. "Our wolves can't nail it down, either, and they're not sure if it's because there's a couple of 'em working together or because there's so many people in and out of there."

Max frowned and Alex's expression mirrored his. "We'll head over, then."

Neal stood and she nearly plopped to the ground on her ass. "I'm going."

"You're staying."

Her mate shook his head. "My mate. My hunt."

Alex glared at him. "And who's going to protect her while we're off chasing these guys down?"

"It could totally be a girl," she grumbled, but was ignored. The 'big boys' were talking.

Ian broke up the fight. "Quit measuring your dicks and focus. You can all go. Dev and I can stay here."

Five sets of eyes turned on her brother and she bristled at their doubt, but Neal ended the potential fight before it began. Ian was not one who tolerated doubt all that well.

"I've seen your sister's shift."

Ian nodded. "So you know that pain is something we're familiar with." Alex flashed her brother a questioning glance and, it seemed that he was going to be accommodating. "Rabbits may be small, cute, and fuzzy little creatures, but how much tolerance for pain do you think I had to develop in order to go from two hundred and twenty-five pounds down to five?"

"It sure as fuck ain't pretty." Neal spoke under his breath.

She whacked him. "It's fucking gorgeous."

He tugged her close. "Of course, angel."

"Patronizing ass." She stuck out her tongue.

"Don't show it if you're not willing to use it."

Carly pushed to her tiptoes and Ian broke into their moment. "Please don't maul my sister in front of me." She glared at her brother. Ian didn't seem to care. "So Dev and I will stay here and the rest of you can go check out what the others have discovered. Call me if you find anything."

Everything decided, the house became a flurry of activity. Neal strapped on a gun, or ten—at least it seemed like it—filled his magazines and secured long-ass knives to his thighs.

The rest of the men were outfitted just like him.

Men and their toys.

Before long, she had Neal looming over her, worry etched in every line of his face. "Be careful."

She snorted. "You be careful. I'm going to watch some TV and worry about you. You're prepared for war."

Neal cupped her cheek, stroked her bottom lip with his thumb. "Not war. Just a 'come to Jesus' meeting." He brushed a soft kiss across her lips. "Stay inside. Listen to Dev and your brother. We're going to follow this trail and get rid of whoever's after you."

Chapter Five

Bored.

Bored. Bored.

Worried.

But still bored.

Had she mentioned bored?

It hadn't even been that long. Twenty minutes, tops, and since they hadn't received a call from the men, she knew they hadn't arrived at the bar yet.

At first, she'd stayed glued to the couch, phone in hand, afraid to move an inch in case one of the males called. That lasted all of five minutes. She didn't do 'worried waiting missus' well.

Her brother and Devlin had searched the house, checked windows, lowered the blinds, and closed the curtains. No sense in making her an easy target, they'd said.

Target. Wow.

All she'd wanted was a mate...a cub...happiness...

Well, she'd gotten the mate and the cub. Happiness was being stubborn as all get out, but she figured she'd get it someday.

Carly pulled her legs onto the couch, wiggled and shifted until she could lie down, and then plopped the phone onto her chest. Letting out a slow, deep breath, she closed her eyes. She might as well relax while she could. No telling when the guys would call in with news. Then again, if Alex's lions and Max's wolves couldn't scent the culprit, she wasn't sure how the big bad leaders could do any better.

Whatever.

Okay, not whatever. She was worried, terrified, and anxious. Somewhere out there lurked a homicidal freak who wanted her dead for one reason or another. Hell, based on what the guys had said, it could even be groups of crazies.

Carly still thought it was the psycho-bitch, Naomi.

Seriously.

"Okay, little bit?"

She smiled at hearing her nickname on Ian's lips. "Yeah, Ian. I'm fine."

"The kit?"

She opened one of her eyes a crack. "Does everyone know?"

He just grinned and she recognized a bit of young Ian, the boy she'd known before he'd had the mantle of being the warren's Buck thrust upon him. "Everyone that knows you and knows your scent. You've got a bit of sunshine added in now." Ian snagged her hand and held it in the cradle of his palms, eyes serious while he stared at her. "Are you happy, little bit?"

Carly slid her free hand over her abdomen to rest on her lower stomach, thinking of the tiny life growing inside her. "I am."

"You sure you're good with that cat? I know you've been...hesitant about him."

She snorted. Couldn't help it. "That's putting it mildly. I dug in my heels so deep I thought I'd end up in China." She sighed. "But he loves me and I refuse to let him off easy and tell him that I love him. I need to make him sweat a bit."

That comment got her a wide grin from her brother. "That's my girl."

"I know, right? I figure I'll make him suffer a little more and then pounce and sex him up—"

Ian dropped her hand so fast, she thought maybe he'd caught fire. Opening her eyes wider, she watched him clap his palms over his ears. "La la la, I'm not listening. Sex and my sister do not go into the same sentence." He glared at her. "Ever."

Carly raised a single brow and smirked at him. "And what do you think I used to do during the Gaian Moon?"

"I pretended you didn't exist."

She stuck out her tongue and blew a raspberry. "Pft on you."

"Pft on me?" Ian narrowed his eyes. "Don't make me freeze all your accou—"

"Children?" They turned their attention to Devlin. "Looks like we might have some company. Car's coming up the driveway." That really got their attention and they swiveled their heads toward Dev and watched as he kept low, gun in hand, and peered through the covered window. "Small four door, dark. One person behind the wheel, but that doesn't mean others aren't hiding in there."

The gravel crunched and shifted as the car drew nearer.

"Do you really think people trying to kill me would be that stupid?"

Ian pushed from the coffee table and crouched beside her, tugging her from the couch. He pulled her through the room, down the hall, and back toward Neal's bedroom. Without a word, he yanked her into the master bathroom, pushed her into the tub, and then gave her a glare that told her he'd gladly kill her himself if she moved an inch.

So she stayed put.

Mostly.

Okay, not really.

The second she thought she was safe (from Ian, not the visitor) she crawled from the tub and crept through her mate's room, skirted the big-assed bed, and then squatted near the window, back against the wall. She twitched the corner of the curtain aside and peered into the darkness. The lights on the vehicle disappeared and she watched as a single person emerged.

She totally knew that silhouette!

"It's Andrew! Don't shoot him!" She popped to her feet and raced through the house, worried that Ian and Devlin would kill her best guy friend. Then again, she wasn't sure why she was a big ball of worry since he *was* part of their warren and her brother was sure to recognize the male. Hopefully. But the guys had seemed uber twitchy, so better safe than sorry.

"Damn it, Carly!" Huh. Her brother could almost roar as loud as Neal.

She dodged her brother and thumped right into Devlin.

"Carly." Oh. His growl was almost scary.

Ha! As if.

"It's just Andrew." She pouted.

Carly could hear her brother's grumble about dumb sisters and tying them to trees, but ignored him. He'd only gotten the jump on her that one time and she'd been five...

A quick knock interrupted their glare-down and Ian trudged toward the front door. The locks gave way with a few flicks and then the door swung wide to reveal...

"Andrew!" Gawd. If she had to be kept on house arrest, even if it was for her own good, at least she'd have a friend with her. She rushed forward and wrapped her arms around his neck in a fierce hug. "Thank God you're here. I'm so bored."

Her friend raised a single brow. "You became bored in all of twenty minutes?"

Carly narrowed her eyes. "I hate you."

"Naw, you love me." He grinned at her, but it didn't quite meet his eyes and she knew she was partly responsible for that look.

They'd been Tweedledum and Tweedledee for so long, the last six months had to have been hard on him. When Carly hadn't been mooning over her mate, or railing against him for his slutty behavior, she'd been holed up with Maya and eating enough ice cream to fill the ocean. Thank God for shifter metabolism. At least she hadn't gotten fatter than she already was.

She looped her arm through his and tugged him toward the hall and Neal's bedroom. Not the best place to take another male, but she wanted to talk without her brother nearby.

"Carly…" Ian's voice trailed after them.

She ignored him. The best part of being the buck's sister was that she could resist his growls. Hard to fear a man that she'd seen naked since she was three.

Two steps into the bedroom, she kicked the door shut.

"Save me." She stumbled toward the bed and pretended to faint, falling onto the soft surface with a bounce.

"Carls…" A frown marred Andrew's sweet, little boy face. The man was nearing thirty and still looked fifteen.

She stared at the white popcorn ceiling. "I know this isn't funny. It's dumb and scary and did I tell you I'm pregnant?" She waved a hand. "Never mind, you probably know already. I smell different, apparently." Carly stacked her hands behind her head. "So, who do you think wants to kill me?"

For a while, Andrew didn't say a word, but she didn't rush him. He was a thinker and tended to work things through in his head before voicing his ideas. Seconds ticked by and finally he lay down next to her, shoulder to shoulder, hip to hip. He shifted and wiggled a little next to her, probably getting comfortable, but still he remained silent.

"Who wants to kill you? Hmm..."

She tilted her head to the side and nudged his head with hers. "Yeah. I think it's that Naomi bitch. The growly guys think its Freedom or HSE, but I still vote for the skinny whore."

Andrew wiggled again. Sometimes the man couldn't get comfortable.

"No, I don't think its Naomi. Though she could be involved somehow. There could be more at play than they realize."

"No? You think she's had help?" That wasn't something she'd ever considered, but Carly couldn't discount her friend's opinion.

"Maybe..." He sighed and turned toward her. "You know I love you, Carly, right?"

She internally winced, knowing that the love he confessed was romantic and not friendly. "I know."

"Good, because I love you and I'm doing this for you. You'll see, it'll be so much better this way." A sharp pinch hit her, the stinging hint of pain emanating from her forearm and she winced. "All along, it's been me."

Well, that sucked. She'd totally kick his ass...the second she woke up...

* * *

What could have been minutes, or hours, later, Carly awoke.

Mostly.

Maybe.

A piercing throb invaded her head, pounding in time with her heart, but she couldn't let the pain overtake her. Nope, she had some business to attend to.

Namely, kicking Andrew's ass.

She slitted her eyelids, taking stock of her position. She was in a small, one-room cabin, arms tied behind her back and a cloth over her mouth. How trite. Really? Andrew couldn't have gotten a little creative with the kidnapping? Whatever. When *she* planned an abduction, she'd go all out with the secret holding location. Something super advanced and technology-y.

Further inspection of the room revealed the skinny psycho bitch (aka Naomi) tied similarly to her along the opposite wall. Her eyes were wide, the whites nearly glowing in the dim interior, and her nostrils flared with each quick exhale. She huffed and puffed like a freight train, and Carly could smell her panic, the acidy tang flicking her nose.

Blech.

While carnivores were all about having fun with the panic stricken prey, herbivores were just turned off. Actually, the feeling made Carly's rabbit run as far away as she could, not wanting to get caught up in a predator's blood thirst. Cause as sure as God made dandelions, a carnivore saw panicking prey as a tasty meal.

Carly was not a tasty meal. Nope. Never. Unless it was Neal and he was between her thighs...

A shuffle to her left drew her attention and she watched a body in the shadows move around the kitchen. Based on the size and build, she figured it was her kidnapper, Andrew.

God.

Andrew.

He'd been her best guy friend for what seemed like forever. He was always at her side, all smiles and laughs, and he'd gotten along famously with Maya and Beth.

And he wanted her dead.

An ache built in her heart, filled it with pain and anger.

He'd killed Beth.

Shot at her.

And now, he'd filled her with drugs.

What would come next?

A whisper-soft whimper from Naomi drew his attention and Carly trailed after him with her eyes. The man she thought she knew spun on his heel and stomped toward his other captive, pulled his leg back and let it fly. Naomi's muffled cry filled the room and a flare of compassion flickered to life. The woman was probably involved in Andrew's plot in some way, but humans were delicate and Carly could only imagine the damage he'd just done.

Well, this had been what he'd meant by 'mostly'. Naomi had to have been involved in some way.

"Stupid bitch. Be quiet. I want my mate to sleep a little longer." He was crazy. Certifiable. "She'll need her rest before we get rid of that little brat she's carrying." His attention strayed to Carly and she couldn't keep still any longer; she opened her eyes and growled low, hissed at Andrew. "Ah, sweetheart, don't be like that." Her friend approached, boots clunking and thumping against the wood floor, and squatted before her. "I forgive you for mating with that cat. At first I wanted you dead for betraying me, and my new friend agreed. He told me how to do it all, showed me where to go. Gave me my first opportunity... I tried again, but then the bullets didn't hit home and I changed my mind and decided to keep you." He licked his lips and she could sense the nervousness building in him. "I just need to convince him that it's better if you live. Right. Better..."

Her ex-friend stroked her head, fingers sifting through her hair, and she jerked away from his touch, glaring. If only looks could kill... "Aw, dear heart. Don't be that way." He traced the line of her nose and tapped the end. "I'm sure I can convince him to be happy with Naomi's death. After all, a human dying at the hands of a shifter is sure to put the government in an uproar. Now she can die instead of you..." A disgruntled yell came from Naomi and Andrew stomped toward to her, reared his leg back, and delivered a fierce kick.

Leaving the other woman groaning, he came back to Carly. "Now, where was I? Oh." He looked thoughtful for a moment, a soft ghosting of regret passing across his features. "I am sad about Bethy. She was such a sweet girl." He rolled to his feet and placed his hands on his hips. "But that can't be helped. Except, then it all got so mucked up." He rubbed his brow. "Naomi saw me shoot at you, you know.

I got my hands on her and then I kept watch on the lion's house. It was so easy to get you out once most of them left. So easy..." Andrew jerked his head, shaking it quickly and then seemed to refocus. "So we'll leave her in your place. It'll be perfect... I hope he doesn't make me keep with our original plans, though." His fingers settled on his temples and he massaged his forehead. "I hope... I hope... I hope..."

Asshole. Demented asshole. Asshole, motherfucker, cocksucker, piece of shit—

The rumble of an approaching engine drew his attention and Carly strained to hear what the hell was going on.

She poked at her internal rabbit, the near-feral animal aching to rip out Andrew's throat, no questions asked. She did her best to soothe the bunny's ruffled fur, assure her that they'd taste his blood, but first they needed to figure out all of the players in the game. Who he fuck was 'he'?

Sure, she had jealous Andrew in front of her, but this new arrival, Andrew's mysterious 'friend'... *that* had her worried.

If it'd been Neal and the rest of the big, bad leaders, they wouldn't have driven right up to the front door, which meant this guy...he was yet another piece of the fucked up puzzle.

Part of her felt bad for Naomi. Almost. Okay, mostly. The woman had been at the wrong place at the wrong time and now she'd suffer for that simple twist of fate.

Rabbit now playing her part, Carly strained to hear, but all she could catch were the murmur of voices; the newcomer's was soft and deep, cutting off Andrew whenever he uttered a sound.

A heavier tread entered the one-room cabin and Carly felt her first wave of fear as the man's scent was carried on the cool air of the AC.

Polar bear. Big, short-fused, evil polar bear. They were notorious for killing first and *not* asking questions later.

Fuckity fuck fuck.

Carly rolled back a bit, struggling to see the new arrival. She didn't have to wait long. In moments the huge man came into view and, oh shit, she was totally dead.

He was taller than Alex—wider, too—with muscles that had muscles that had muscles. Dressed in all black from head to toe, he looked like a man most would run from without hesitation. He had a wicked long scar running from hairline to collar bone, the wide swath of his white injury simply adding to the air of danger that surrounded him.

For the first time in her life, she felt pure terror; the fear pounded through her blood stream until she couldn't breathe.

The newcomer squatted before her, his long black hair falling forward as he stared down at her tied form. "Hello, pretty. You've caused me a bit of grief, you know. You were supposed to die tonight, but I can see that Andrew had a bit of trouble doing his job." He reached behind him, hand out of sight for barely a moment, before it returned with a ten-inch knife, the sharp blade glistening in the dim light. "It's not a problem, though."

* * *

Neal was ready to tear his hair out. They'd just pulled into the parking lot when he got the call.

Andrew had taken Carly right from underneath their noses.

Pressing the 'end call' button on his cell, he wasn't surprised when his thumb cracked the screen.

"He's got her."

The males stomping across the graveled parking lot of Honey's Bar stilled and turned back toward him.

Alex was the first to speak, voice deadly. "Who's got whom?"

"Andrew." The lion surged forward, stalked him just beneath his skin, muscles and bones bunched in preparation for a fight. "Ian and Devlin let him in because he's her friend and part of the warren. And now he's kidnapped her." The cat wanted to tear something to shreds. Preferably the male who had dared touch what belonged to him. "The male snuck her out the window and shoved her into his car. Drove away before they even knew she'd been abducted. Ian is researching the rabbit's assets to see if there's somewhere he'd take her. Somewhere..."

"It's not just that bunny, Neal." The voice came from the darkness, but he recognized the male with ease. He'd been 'vacationing' in Ridgeville for the last six months or so and was a well-known tracker for the council, a man who went after feral shifters and dangerous Freedom members.

He was also one of the most dominant and dangerous males he'd ever met. The guy had been nice enough during the visit, but this was something...different. Dominance, anger, and power radiated from the male in giant waves that he couldn't help but recognize.

The tiger was *pissed*.

"Ricker." Neal tilted his head to the side, not anxious to anger the man. He heard a murmured echo of the tiger's name from those behind him and assumed the others were mimicking his movement.

The cat stalked forward, feet not making a sound on the loose gravel, body moving like the ultimate predator, and Neal couldn't suppress the slivers of fear that entered his blood. This man could end Neal within the blink of an eye and there were whispers that the male wouldn't hold an ounce of remorse for the act.

"I know who has her and I know where she is."

"Where?"

"Who?" Alex's voice drowned out his.

"One-room cabin near Crest Lake. As for who, it started with her friend, Andrew, but it's truly…" The tiger's eyes, deep golden amber, bore into his. "Alistair McCain."

* * *

Oh shit, oh god, oh shit, oh god… The blade inched closer and closer to her face and she couldn't do a damned thing about it. Honestly, she wasn't all that concerned about him slicing the vulnerable skin and leaving her with scars… Nope, her biggest worry was that he wouldn't stop there.

"Alistair." Andrew stepped into her line of sight. "I changed my mind. I want to keep her. We'll kill Naomi, make it look like shifters, and then Carly and I can disappear and—"

Her enemy—yet still somehow her friend—didn't get the rest of his words out. Nope, not before Alistair spun on the balls of his feet quicker than she could blink and shoved that deadly blade into Andrew just below his breastbone and straight up into the man's heart. Shock was stuck on her friend's features, his eyes and mouth open wide. A brief look of regret flashed across his face just before the vacant stare of death took over.

That fast. A blink. A heartbeat. That's all it took for the male to end Andrew's life. No hesitation, no wonder or arguing. Just death. Period. Full stop.

The big motherfucker slid the knife free of Andrew's body and then turned his attention back to her, wiping the blade clean on her jeans and coating her in her friend's fluids.

"Sorry about that, lovely. Now, let me introduce myself. I'm Alistair McCain and you are our first step to freedom."

Alistair McCain. Leader of Freedom and a bad-assed, 'fuck you and die' polar bear. Freedom's only focus was destroying the communal structure shifters had operated under since the beginning of time. They wanted the council abolished and Alphas, Primes and all other leaders destroyed. According to them, shifters were fine on their own and they didn't need anyone telling them what to do or how to live their lives.

She was dead. Deader than dead. A ghost walking—er, laying. It was only a matter of time before...

A whimper from across the room drew Alistair's attention away from her and Carly was torn in two. She could draw the man's anger onto herself or let Naomi suffer next.

Decisions, decisions...

Oh, who the fuck was she kidding. Naomi may have been a bitch, but she hadn't done anything 'wrong', per se.

Drawing one leg back, she brought it forward as hard as she could and kicked Alistair in the ass, knocking him to the floor before he could get to the evil bitch and use his Ginsu on her.

"Fucking cunt!" The male roared and spun back to her, a pale white hint of fur covering his features, the lines of his cheeks and chin sharper than before. "Are you ready for death, little one? Is that it?" He reached for her and yanked at her gag, tugged it free of her mouth. "Will you scream for me while I gut you?"

"Fuck you." She spat at him, a glob of saliva landing on his chiseled cheek.

Stupid, but at least he wasn't bearing down on Naomi.

"Ah, lovely, how you tempt me. Perhaps I should sample you first." The bastard grasped her chin with a bruising hold and held her still, licked her face from chin to brow. "How sweet you taste." His voice was a deep growl and she could smell his arousal, the perverted need in him. Another lap at her skin. "So lovely."

Alistair released her and changed position, shifting so that she could stare into Naomi's fear painted eyes. The human didn't move, barely breathed, while the fucker sliced through Carly's top, the long blade cutting through the fabric like butter. Soon, the cool air of the cabin sent goose bumps over her skin, and his next cut rendered her bra useless. Her breasts were bared to the room and she chanced a look at Alistair's features only to turn her attention from him again.

Lust, pure and simple.

Depraved fucker. Just wait until she was free of the ropes. She'd let her little claws come out to play so she could slice and dice his balls.

Yeah, that sounded like a fuck-ton of fun.

"Look at those pretty nipples." He grasped them between his fingers and pinched, harder and harder until tears formed in her eyes and slid down her cheeks. But she wouldn't make a sound. No, she figured he took enjoyment in others' pain and she wasn't about to help him get his rocks off. He twisted, increasing the pressure, and she breathed deeply through her nose, great puffing breaths heaved in and out of her lungs while she bore the pain.

The rabbit inside her growled and reared, chomped on air, desperate to get the male's hands off of her. Alistair wasn't her *mate*. He had no *right* to touch her. Ever.

With a growl, he released her and then turned his attention further down her body, eyes resting at the juncture of her thighs. She'd die first. Truly.

Alistair brandished the wicked blade, edge gleaming, and brought it to the button of her jeans. Again, it parted the fabric near the fastener like a hot knife through butter, the cloth melting away with barely a touch. More and more of her was revealed and she cringed when his fingers glided over the skin of her lower belly. "That's lovely."

Carly shimmied and wiggled, tugged and tore at her bonds. No. She wouldn't let him do this to her. God, she couldn't breathe, couldn't think, couldn't do anything but fight. Her rabbit, all for getting the hell away from this fucker, urged her on, shoved forward and became desperate for the change.

She let a little of the furball's power slither through the walls that kept her bunny at bay. In a blink, the rabbit pushed, yanked control, and forced her wrists and hands to change.

While the pain of a partial change tore through her, she kicked at Alistair, nailed him in the thigh and then again between his legs.

The male roared and reached for her jeans, tore them from her body, exposed her. With his grab, her panties followed, leaving her bare from the waist down.

The rabbit helped her then, got her wrists free of her bindings with a quick slice of her claws, releasing her arms. Hands free, she used them to brace her as she struck out with her leg again, fighting with all that she had. Alistair staggered back a step.

Taking advantage of the distraction, she scrambled for the knife, crawled and clawed until the handle of the ten-inch blade rested against her palm.

Hand wrapped around the hilt, a roar of triumph grew in her chest. But it was short-lived. A scream erupted when searing hot, near debilitating pain roared through her hip and leg. She was flipped over, Alistair's shifted claws digging into her flesh, slicing through the fat and muscle of her body. Without thought, she struck out with the blade, cut and carved at his hands and arms, uncaring of any damage she may have caused to herself. She wouldn't be raped by his filth, and refused to let the demented male take her kit from her.

Another swipe and she caught his face, the blade traveling over one cheek, across his nose, and then against the other cheek. Now he had a new scar to go with the other.

"Bitch." He pulled one claw free and then sunk it in again, gripping her waist and tugging her toward him, wicked nails cutting down to the bone.

Alistair bared his fangs, saliva dripping from his extended canines and dropping against her exposed skin. She sliced at him again, repeating the move yet the man didn't seem to notice. She gave him another cut, even deeper and Alistair snarled in response, his jaw elongating to resemble the polar bear he held inside his body.

The male froze, body half over her, Carly's blood pouring from her wounds, and he tilted his head to the side. "It sounds as if the cavalry has arrived. Apparently the sniveling male did not do very well." He released her in an instant, claws retracting from her flesh, and he rose to his full height. The rabbit wanted to jump to her feet, cut and claw at the male, destroy him. She'd kill him or die trying. "Until we meet again."

With that simple goodbye, he melted from the room, leaving Carly alone with the pale-faced, white-eyed Naomi and her ex-friend's body.

Damn, but she wished she could bring Andrew back so she could take a piece out of his hide.

Carly breathed deep, chest heaving and heart struggling with every beat. The minute she woke up, she'd figure out a way to bring Andrew back from the dead so she could kill him again.

She just needed a *tiny* nap first.

* * *

Six hours later, Neal was still shaking, lion pacing inside his mind, stalking back and forth while he fought the urge to join Ricker's hunt for Alistair McCain. He battled the urge to snarl at the thought of the man's name.

He couldn't do anything while he waited for Carly to heal. Her injuries were severe, deep enough to reveal bone, and the blood loss was staggering. He only hoped that the cub had survived. He knew his mate would have been devastated with the loss of their young, and he wanted to spare her that news.

Neal traced each of her delicate fingers, noticing the pale hue of her skin, and he could see the blue of her veins within. God, he'd almost lost her to the jealousy and the destructive plans of an insane male.

Freedom. He snarled.

Alistair had preyed on Andrew's demented feelings and convinced the male that Carly's death would be the answer to his prayers. No one would have the female that belonged to him.

Instead, Andrew had ended up dead, and Naomi...

"You know she'll be fine. Little Bit's always bounced back." Ian joined him, standing tall at the end of the bed. "Did she tell you about the time she got caught by a fox?"

Neal turned to him, eyes wide. "You're joking."

His mate's brother shook his head. "Nope. She'd gotten mad at our mother, shifted, and ran off into the woods. She'd been gone for an hour or so, our parents frantic, before she came hopping back, bloodied from head to toe and dragging that fucking fox behind her. At seven she informed our mother that foxes did not play fair."

Carly stirred, muscles twitching and legs shifting beneath the thin fabric of the sheet covering her and he stroked her hand, trailed his fingers over her cheek. "Shh, I've got you. You're safe."

Ian's hand rested on his shoulder. "She's tough, cat. By morning she'll be ready to hunt down Andrew and skin him alive. Not that there'll be anything left of the body, since we'll burn it, but she'll still try and figure out a way."

God, Neal hoped so. He could deal with an angry, vengeful Carly any day.

A knock on the bedroom door yanked their attention and they found Alex standing in the hallway. Smart man. Neal wasn't sure he could tolerate an unrelated male near his woman right then.

"We need you two in the living room. Ricker would like a word. Neal, Maya will stay with Carly until you return." With that, Prime disappeared and the *very* pregnant Maya waddled into the room, worry etched into every line of her face.

Neal rose from his chair and stepped aside. The woman toddled even faster and practically fell into the seat he'd vacated. She snatched up Carly's still hand. "You utter bitch. You go on another adventure without me? I bet we coulda sliced and diced that ass. Remember when..."

He smiled at Prima's railing and turned to follow Ian out of the room. His mate would be well cared for by her best friend. Now he had other things to deal with, and he was anxious to hear what the council's tracker had to say.

In the living room, Alex and Ricker waited for them; Max and his enforcer had left as soon as they'd seen the cats and rabbits home. They didn't want to leave their wolves alone while Alistair was in the area and Neal couldn't blame them.

Ricker sat in one of the chairs, elbows resting on his knees. He'd been hunting for hours and looked exhausted. "I lost him on the other side of the lake. Fucker hopped into an SUV and took off. There were tracks of at least three others, but I caught the scent of another two that had probably stayed in the vehicle. A hard scent of fear hung around, which means they've either got a reluctant Freedom member or they have their hands on someone else."

Neal clenched his hands, fought the urge to shift and roar, take off into the wilderness and hunt the bastard, the leader of Freedom.

His mate. *His mate* had been hurt.

He ached for the death of every member of that fucking organization. He wanted the blood of Freedom members to flow in rivers so that they couldn't hurt anyone else.

Ever.

The tracker stood and ran a hand through his hair. "I'll be gone as soon as I pack my stuff. The council staff are running the tire treads and checking on recent rentals. I'm going to ground for now and waiting to see if there's any whispers."

"What about Naomi?" God, she was crazed after what she'd been through. Her body had been battered, bruised, and broken in several places, but she was human. Knowing enough about shifters to have sex with them and bear their cubs was one thing...seeing the violence they were capable of was another.

He didn't know how she'd fare or what to tell the kids just yet. He wasn't sure if he should lie or tell the truth...their mother wouldn't be the same, either way.

Ricker crossed his arms over his massive chest. "It's your call. She'll be damaged, maybe permanently, and she knows a lot about y'all. More than the average human. As far as the council is concerned, it's an internal matter unless she starts talking."

Neal nodded, quickly followed by the other two males, and Ricker seemed to relax. The male probably had enough of dispensing judgment on others and he apparently didn't want to be saddled with a human's future. "Good." He jerked his head in a quick nod. "I hope to never see you again. At least, not when blood's involved."

He shook the male's hand, Ian and Alex repeating the gesture in turn, but Alex held fast. "You are always welcome on our land and in our pride, Ricker. We won't ever forget this. If you decide to retire, you have a home in Ridgeville."

Neal watched the tiger stride from the house and, while his lion was respectfully fearful of the huge beast, a part of him couldn't help but be sad at the male's departure. Their pride would be stronger with him in it. Maybe...

Maya's voice cut into his thoughts. "Neal? She's asking for you." The woman smirked. "And when I say 'asking', I mean ready to gnaw your ass if you don't get in there ASAP. She said she's horny, hungry, and hormonal from the kit which is your fault. In that order."

Praise Jesus hallelujah amen. She'd live.

Epilogue

Carly would kill him. Really. Tear him limb from limb. Arms, then legs, then cock. Wait. Maybe if she just got rid of the arms and legs, she could still use his cock. Then he wouldn't have a way of defending his manhood. She should Google.

Asshole.

Huge asshole.

She'd healed already. No more pink lines from her wounds. No nightmares. Nada.

Carly was safe, damn it.

Ricker was off hunting Alistair and reports indicated he'd abandoned Ridgeville.

Naomi had been sent on 'vacation'. And by 'vacation', she meant a mental health facility. After being captured by Andrew and Alistair, the human woman had a few 'issues'.

With a sigh, she fell into bed. Alone. She'd waited for him last night, all naked and ready...and had fallen asleep. The coward had waited for her to pass out. That had to be the only explanation.

Argh.

"Cccaaarrrlllyyy!" Aw, little—but very loud—Elijah was up. Carly found Neal's kids adorable, but her mate had assured her that her opinion would change after more than a handful of days. With Naomi 'on vacation', they'd welcomed the cubs into their home and Carly couldn't remember why she'd been so upset about their existence. Part of her wished that their mother never got better. Only a little part. Teeny, even.

Maybe.

"Cccaaawwwyyy!" Carson echoed his older brother.

A loud, roaring cry rent the air, which meant that baby Ryan was up, as well. Whew, that boy took after his daddy.

With a groan, she rolled from the bed and snagged her robe. Neal was probably up and feeding the cubs, so she could relax for a bit, but she enjoyed joining them all in a raucous breakfast.

She padded through the house and into the kitchen to find her men surrounding the table. Both Elijah and Carson fed themselves (mostly) while Neal spooned wet cereal into Ryan's mouth as he sat in his high chair.

"How are my boys?" She got four smiles in response.

Moving around the room, she dropped a soft kiss on the top of each little head and gave Neal something that was nowhere near chaste. Her male moaned, but quickly pulled away, glaring at her with a frown.

Butthole. She'd keep teasing until he gave in.

A rapid knock of knuckles against wood came from the front of the house and she waved Neal away when he began to rise. "I've got it. Keep making sure they all eat." Carly wasted no time in answering the door, revealing Maya and Alex waiting for her. "'Morning."

"Hey. We're here to rescue you." Maya smiled wide.

She raised a brow at Alex. "Didn't you do that already?"

He just rolled his eyes. "We're 'borrowing' the kids so that we can get 'practice'."

She turned her attention to Maya. "Translation?"

"We're stealing them so you can *bowchickabowbow* with your mate. I'm tired of hearing you complain." Maya stuck out her tongue.

God, that's why she loved the she-cat.

Opening the door wide, she gestured for them to enter. "By all means. My vagina thanks you."

Maya giggled and Alex looked like he was gonna be sick. Apparently thinking of other women's vaginas didn't agree with the man. What the hell else should she have called it? Pussy? Hell no, she'd never say that to anyone other than her mate.

Her BFF swept past her, Alex trailing behind, and Carly was met with a chorus of "Uncle Alex!" and "Auntie Maya!"

Somehow, in what seemed like mere moments, the three children were spirited away within minutes, leaving just her and Neal in the house.

She was going to seduce him, damn it.

Carly found Neal in the kitchen, table cleared and dishes piled in the sink. He had his back to her, hands moving over the plates and silverware with a soap-coated sponge. Man, she loved a guy who cleaned. She just may keep him.

Tiptoeing across the room, she used all of her sneaky-sneak skills that she had acquired over the years and crept up behind him. She raised her arms, determined to surprise him and enfold him in a hug he wouldn't want to end.

"I can feel you, Carly."

She stopped, planted a hand on her hip and huffed. "You could have played along, you know."

Her mate turned on her, holding a towel as he dried his hands and gave her that smirk she both loved and hated. "But then…" He tossed the towel onto the counter. "I wouldn't have been able to do this."

Neal reached for her, wrapped his strong arms around her waist, and brought her body flush against his.

He dropped his head as they collided, brought his mouth to hers, and seized her with a dominating kiss. He forced his tongue between her lips, tangling it with hers and tasting every part of her. Carly responded in kind, stroked and teased him, explored the parts that she'd forgotten, familiarized herself with her mate once again.

Carly's body responded to his assault, her nipples hardened against the smooth fabric of her robe, the silk tempting her with what would assuredly come. The male was going to fuck her now. Even if she had to tie him to the bed to do it.

Tied to the bed…

She wrapped her arms around his neck, increased the pressure between their mouths, showed him without words how desperate she was. It'd only been a week, but it felt like years.

Neal sucked on her tongue, traced her teeth, taunted her with his intimate kiss. Her body became restless with the possessive torture, pussy growing heavy with every breath, breasts tingling and aching for attention. She craved him like a drug.

She could feel his erection, his hardened cock pressing against her belly, only the material of her robe and his jeans separating them.

Her mate eased the kiss, slowing their tangle, their tasting, and pulled his lips from hers. "Hey, angel."

"Mate." She breathed the word, licked his upper lip, savored that hint of his flavor. "My mate. Need you." She whispered, repeated the action.

She was desperate for him and wasn't afraid to admit it. The male was her perfect partner and she wasn't about to go without him for another second.

Neal growled, wrapped his arms around her, cupped her ass and lifted her with ease. Instinctively, she wrapped her legs around his waist, trusting him to support her. He strode across the kitchen and into the hallway.

Carly couldn't wait to taste him again, though. She nipped and sucked on his neck, spring rain and daffodils burst across her tongue and a tortured groan came from deep within her mate's chest. With a *thud*, her back hit the wall and she was held suspended between his body and the hard surface behind her.

"Pants. Pants, pants, pants..." His voice was barely recognizable, but she got the gist of his demand. After all, she was all for his jeans disappearing from between her thighs and his thick cock taking their place.

Snagging her mate's lips in another desperate kiss, she wiggled her hands between their bodies, fought with the button on his pants and came out the victor. A rip and shove had his dick leaping into her hand, the fat shaft filling her palm just as she remembered.

Her pussy throbbed in celebration, the memory of him stretching and filling her, sliding in and out of her slick heat. She moaned against his mouth, clawed at his shoulders and pushed herself higher along his body. Hand still clasping his erect dick, she placed the head of his prick at her entrance and then released her hold, allowed her weight to force his invasion.

His cock glided into her moist pussy, her juices easing his way as Neal filled her to bursting. Inch after inch slipped into her waiting hole, slices of pinching pain blossomed into pure pleasure as the head of his dick grazed her G-spot. A shudder of arousal pulsed through her pussy, clit throbbing with the friction of their bodies.

Carly's hiss was echoed by Neal's groan. Her mate lifted her with ease, pussy clinging to his shaft as he forced her heat to release him and then welcome him once again as he lowered her body.

She tore her lips from his, their mouths hovering a hair's breadth apart as she whispered against his lips. "So full. So good."

Neal repeated the movement, lifting her up and down along his hard shaft, stroking out and then back into her waiting, soaked warmth. Her pussy contracted along his length, rippled and throbbed.

"So tight, angel." He withdrew and shoved forward. "So. Fucking. Tight." Each word was punctuated with a fierce thrust.

Carly growled and nipped at his lower lip, laved the droplet of blood that gathered and let his sensual flavors roll over her taste buds.

"Yes! Big. Fuck. More." She grunted and groaned along with him, breasts jiggling with his every move. She shared her mate's breath, both of them unable to do anything more than pant their pleasure as they let their desires loose.

God, even a week had been much too long to go without his sensual touch.

Way too long.

Neal held her steady against the wall, pistoning his thick cock in and out of her now sopping wet pussy. The lewd, wet sounds of their sex filled the small corridor and mixed with their heavy breathing.

Carly's pleasure gained on her; with every shove into her waiting cunt, it ratcheted higher, growing. It encircled her, wrapped around her waist, and then slid down to envelope her pussy. The throbbing ache had grown into a pulsating desperation.

She rocked and rolled her hips against him, encouraged his rough thrusts, the rub of his pelvis against her clit. She clawed and scratched at his exposed chest, urged him to give her more, faster, deeper. She growled and groaned, snarled and hissed as he worked her over, faster and faster.

The *slap, slap, slap* of his hips against hers increased and she embraced the evidence of their lovemaking as ecstasy built and grew inside her, signaling the rapid approach of her release. "Gonna come..."

The pleasure she'd been nurturing was becoming uncontrollable. Her pussy tightened around him in a rough rhythm, cunt filled with bliss as he pummeled her with his cock. More and more he gave her until she thought she'd burst.

"Come on my cock, angel. Give it to me." He groaned and bit her lip in return, drew his own droplets of blood and the spear of pain only served to increase her carnal desire.

Carly dug her nails into his shoulders, claws scarring him, and she reveled in the soul deep growl that sounded from his chest. Her pussy responded to his sounds, pulsed, and pleasure flowed through her. It crept into every nook and cranny of her body, filled her from within, sparked a response from every nerve. Her arms and legs twitched and spasmed, her impending orgasm stealing her control.

"Come... Give it to me and I'll come so deep in you angel...fill you up."

God, the idea of having his cum inside her, painting her from inside out, was the tipping point. The orgasm that had been threatening burst over her, dark spots danced in front of her eyes and she screamed. His name was on her lips, over and over, a chant that seemed to have no end in sight.

Still, his cock continued to slide in and out of her slick passage, her cream coating his dick while he sought his release. His never ending fucking merely brought on another climax, this one harder and more violent than the last.

Hot lava seemed to pour through her veins, pumped faster than a heartbeat and she truly lost control. Carly sunk her teeth into him, a scream on her lips while the ecstasy of her release stole whatever power she had over her body. Twitches and spasms of her muscles went unnoticed as the pleasure invaded her, the molten sensations of climax destroyed her and she was simply a victim of her body's desires.

Neal's thrusts suddenly turned frantic and uneven until he sealed his hips to hers, a roar on his lips as he sunk his teeth deep into her shoulder, marking her for all to see.

She screamed again, more ecstasy pouring into her already sated body while his cock twitched and throbbed deep inside her pussy, doing exactly as he had promised. Her cunt milked his shaft, seeming to crave every drop of his cum.

Panting and exhausted, Carly let her mate support her. Okay, she had to admit, maybe she wasn't all that entirely, perfectly healed, since twinges of pain were making themselves known now that they were done. But she'd die before she admitted it.

She snuggled into Neal's hold and breathed in his musky scent. Damn, how she loved the man. Eek. Love. He'd said it once before, but...she hadn't.

Licking her lips, she raised her head and stared at his features, his strong jaw, straight nose, and prominent brow.

Before she could lose her nerve, she blurted out the truth. "I love you."

He opened one eye. "I know."

"You know?" She smacked him on the chest. "What do you mean, 'I know'?" She bent her head and bit into his shoulder. Not deep; just a pinch of his skin between her teeth. "The right answer is 'I love you, too'."

Neal let his eye close seemingly immune to the pain. "You know I love you, baby."

"You better."

His hand snaked to the back of her head and she let him pull her up, brushing his lips across hers. "More than life itself."

She harrumphed. "Good. 'Cause if you didn't...hell hath no fury..."

"Furry? Or fury?" Neal nipped her lower lip. "Because, you are furry. And soft. In all the most delicious places."

"Fury."

"Not furry?" He quirked a brow, smirk on those luscious lips. "I like you all furry and sweet."

"You're being obtuse on purpose."

"Hmm..." He lapped at her mouth.

The shrill ring of the kitchen phone got them moving, Neal helping her to her feet before he padded back down the hall and answered the call. "'Lo? No... How?" Carly stared at him, worry growing in her belly as she continued to listen, his tone one of panic and worry. "When? Ricker? Good. What can we do?" Roiling concern filled her. There was only one reason Ricker would be involved in anything. Freedom had struck again. Oh, God. "All right. Bye."

Neal turned to her and gripped her shoulders, his eyes boring into hers. "There's no easy way to say this, baby. Alistair has Maddy."

Oh. God. *No.*

The End

About Celia Kyle

Celia Kyle would like to rule the world and become a ninja. As a fallback, she's working on her writing career and giving readers stories that touch their hearts and *ahem* other places.

Visit her online at:

http://celiakyle.com

http://twitter.com/celiakyle

http://facebook.com/celiakyle

http://pinterest.com/celiakyle

http://goodreads.com/celiakyle

If you'd like to be notified of new releases AND get free eBooks, subscribe here: http://einkslingers.com

Copyright Page

Published by Summerhouse Publishing. Ridgeville Series: Volume I: Book 1: He Ain't Lion. Book 1.5: You're Lion. Book 2: Ball of Furry. Copyright © 2013 Celia Kyle. ALL RIGHTS RESERVED. This book contains material protected under International and Federal Copyright Laws and Treaties. Any unauthorized reprint or use of this material is prohibited. No part of this book may be reproduced or transmitted in any form or by any means, electronic or mechanical, including photocopying, recording, or by any information storage and retrieval system without express written permission from the author.

Summerhouse Publishing

http://summerhousepublishing.com

This is a work of fiction. The characters, incidents and dialogues in this book are of the author's imagination and are not to be construed as real. Any resemblance to actual events or persons, living or dead, is completely coincidental.

CPSIA information can be obtained
at www.ICGtesting.com
Printed in the USA
BVHW04s1814230518
517165BV00001B/22/P